What Others Are Saying About JACK PATTERSON

"Jack's storytelling feels as natural as James Patterson's, and the short-chapter setup is the literary answer to Lay's potato chips: you just want one more and before you know it, you've gone through the whole thing."

- **David Bashore**, *The Times-News, Twin Falls, ID*

"J.P. does a fantastic job at keeping you engaged and interested. I look forward to more from this talented author."

- *Aaron Patterson, bestselling author of SWEET DREAMS*

"Patterson has a mean streak about a mile wide and puts his two main characters through quite a horrible ride, which makes for good reading."

- *Richard D., reader*

"Like a John Grisham novel, from the very start I was pulled right into the story and couldn't put the book down. It was as if I personally knew and cared about what happened to each of the main characters. Every chapter ended with so much excitement and suspense I had to continue to read until I learned how it ended, even though it kept me up until 3:00 A.M."

- *Ray F., reader*

Acclaim for DEAD SHOT

"Small town life in southern Idaho might seem quaint and idyllic to some. But when local news gins to uncover a series of strang sticky spider web of deception, tl blown wide open. Told with all t old pro, first-timer Jack Patterson hits one out of the park his first time at bat with Cross Hairs. It's that good."

- ***Vincent Zandri***, *bestselling author of* THE REMAINS

"You can tell Jack knows what it's like to live in the newspaper world, but with Dead Shot, he's proven that he also can write one heck of a murder mystery. With a clever plot and characters you badly want to succeed, he is on his way to becoming a new era James Patterson."

- **Josh Katzowitz**,
NFL writer for CBSSports.com & author of
Sid Gillman: Father of the Passing Game

DEAD LINE

A Novel

JACK PATTERSON

DEAD LINE
Electronic Edition Copyright © 2012 Jack Patterson

Print ISBN: 978-1-938848-544

First Print Edition 2011
Second Print Edition 2014

Cover Design by Dan Pitts

Published in the United States of America

Hangman Books
Boise, Idaho 83713

For the 12ᵗʰ Man

"Journalism will kill you, but it will keep you alive while you're at it."

- Horace Greeley

CHAPTER 1

NOAH LARSON WATCHED RAINDROPS cascading down the window over the kitchen sink, racing to a predictable end. Most drops would find their way to the bottom of the sill before joining others to form a small stream that spilled into a dormant flowerbed. A few lucky ones would take control of their fate, resisting the urge to be like all the others by clinging ever so tenuously to an open spot on the glass. But even they were susceptible to being washed away by a collision with just another raindrop or a blast of air. It was a depressing thought, but momentary when the reality of Noah's life collided with it. Who had time to ponder the depths of existentialism when there was a Super Bowl to win?

In three hours, Noah was scheduled to join his teammates on a charter flight to Houston where the Seattle Seahawks would attempt to bring home the city's first Lombardi Trophy. And it was going to happen—he just knew it. Nothing could stop destiny. Ever since he began playing peewee football, Noah's talents were apparent to everyone, including himself. He had boxes of personal trophies, plaques and accolades stored in unmarked containers on a shelf in his garage to prove it. The only trophy Noah wanted to show off was the smooth silver one, hoisted above his head while confetti rained down from the rafters of Gillette Stadium. That destiny was only six days away.

"Dad, did you pack my lunch?" came the question from across the kitchen. Noah snapped back to the present.

"Sure, Jake. Got it right here." The pro quarterback handed his six-year-old son a Spiderman lunch box. "I even remembered to put your favorite Capri Sun in there, too."

"Apple?"

"I thought you liked grape."

"Daaaaad! You always mix up my favorite flavors. I like grape jelly but apple juice."

"Well, we can fix that right now."

Noah shuffled to the pantry and ripped open a six-pack of apple-flavored Capri Suns, grabbing one for Jake.

"Here you go, son. I'll get it right next time—don't you worry."

"It's OK, dad." The first grader stuffed the juice carton into his lunch box. "You know, I'm really gonna miss you this week."

"I'm gonna miss you too, sport. But I'll see you on Friday. You and mom are flying down and we'll do something fun when I'm not busy."

"I can't wait! Can we go see the Dynamo's stadium while we're down there?"

"The Dynamo? Son, I'm playing in the Super Bowl on Sunday and you want to go see an empty soccer stadium?"

"Aww, dad. Soccer is cool, too. Maybe if you win, the Seahawks can have a parade just like the Sounders did when they won the MLS Cup."

Noah tried not to let his son's remark bother him. Jake loved soccer and preferred using his dad's celebrity status to rub shoulders with the city's star soccer players rather than visit the NFL locker room. What gnawed at Noah the most was the fact that Seattle threw a parade befitting of royalty when the city's pro soccer team won the championship the previous fall. The cash-strapped city never dreamed another title might come so soon. But if the Seahawks won, forget budget restraints. Seattle would have a Super Bowl champion and it would celebrate.

Noah knew the city would go into debt in six days to throw a matching parade. He cared less about competing with the city's other pro sports teams but more about the overall sense of despair hovering over Seahawk fans' mentality. Doom and gloom held season tickets for the Seahawks—all 67,000 of them. Noah would change all that, maybe even turn his son into a die-hard football fan in the process.

"Don't worry, son. You can ride with me in the parade next week after we come back home with a trophy."

"Go, Seahawks! Beat the Dolphins!" Jake pumped his fist in the air and without reservation, sprinted across the kitchen to give his dad a high-five. They both laughed. Noah picked his son up and spun him around once. They shared a hug that ended with a tight squeeze.

"Don't forget your rain coat, buddy. It looks like you're going to need it."

"Thanks, Dad."

"Better hurry before you miss your bus."

"Dad, you're beginning to sound like mom."

On cue, Ellen Larson wobbled down the stairs, trying to stay upright in her four-inch stiletto heels. Her naturally blonde hair clung smoothly to her head as her usually flowing locks were twisted into a tight bun and held in place with a diamond-studded hair stick. She wore the shimmering red dress well, which outlined the contours of her curvaceous figure. The silk shawl draped over her shoulders toned down the image of a woman that would put most men's head on a swivel.

Noah drew out a long whistle and shook his head in delight as he watched his wife of eight years come down the staircase. Who cared if she wasn't the most graceful woman at the moment? Noah certainly didn't. And neither did Jake.

"Jake, don't think you're going to school without giving mommy a kiss."

Jake didn't wait for his mother to make it to the front door. He liked being the first kid to arrive at the bus stop and wasn't going to let the obligatory kiss from his mom prevent him from achieving his daily goal.

"I love you, Mommy," Jake planted a wet kiss on her cheek.

"I'll pick you up from school today and then we'll go shopping. We need to get some warm clothes for our trip."

"OK, Mom. See you then."

Ellen went to plant a kiss on Jake's cheek, but he dodged and resisted. If there was one thing that was sure to get a first-grade boy laughed at, it was having bright red lipstick on your cheek. Instead of getting her way, Ellen withdrew and blew a kiss. Jake's face lit up with a toothy grin as he put on his raincoat, grabbed his book bag, and ran toward the door.

The large number of students living in the Larsons' neighborhood who attended Westminster Prep necessitated a school bus. Jake's walk to the bus stop for the city's most prestigious prep school was less than a block. Noah and Ellen had no reservations about letting their son walk alone to the corner of this quiet, tree-lined street. Even on a day that registered as extra blustery and rainy by Seattle's sopping wet standards.

Noah watched Jake pull the door shut and hustle down the steps. Once Jake reached the sidewalk, Noah could see Jake tossing his Sounders soccer ball in the air as he skipped toward the bus stop. Noah craned his neck to watch Jake until he disappeared from his field of view. Noah smiled and shook his head, proud of his little guy.

"Don't you look nice, Ellen," Noah spun around and turned his gaze toward his wife.

"Thanks, honey. I am going to miss you. I can't wait for Sunday to get here and this season to be over with. It's so much better when you lose and don't make the playoffs."

Noah moved closer to Ellen. He put his hands on her shoulders and looked her in the eyes.

"I don't know how to respond to that. Wouldn't you rather be married to a Super Bowl champion quarterback to impress all your socialite friends?"

"I don't care about that—I just want you to be done with football so we can enjoy life together again. This football stuff just gets in the way all the time."

"Well, we'll see."

Ellen suddenly grabbed Noah's arms.

"Seriously? Are you going to retire from football?"

"Well, I've been playing football for a long time, living up to a lot of people's expectations and doing what everyone else thinks I should do. I'm kind of tired of it. Besides, what better way to go out than on top and be the king of this city?"

Ellen began shaking Noah, giddy with excitement. She was careful not to jump up and down in her unstable shoes.

"I can't believe this!"

"I was hoping you would react like this. Honestly, I'd like for this to be the last game I play and go out with a Super Bowl win. It's time."

Ellen smiled.

"You're not just going to win," she said, poking Noah in the chest, "you're going to destroy the Dolphins!"

She turned and headed back upstairs to finish primping for her shopping outing. Noah watched her put her fist in the air and mumble something about "no more football." He knew retiring would make her happy—and it was time to make it official.

Noah glanced at his packed bags by the door. He then walked back to the kitchen and resumed raindrop watching. Noah stared out the window, grappling with the fact that he had uttered aloud the thought that had been tormenting him for the past six months: *Did he have the nerve to walk away from the game that had consumed his entire life?* But there was no going back now. Ellen had likely already committed to memory their entre conversation, word for word. And Noah knew she would make sure he kept his word. It was one of the things he liked best about being married to Ellen. It was also one of the worst.

* * *

CARLOS RIVERA NURSED THE cup of coffee in his right hand. It wasn't cold yet but it was getting there quickly. Another minute or two and it would be undrinkable. Not that he minded. He thought the claim that Seattle was home to the best coffee in the United States was a *chiste*. It had been a week since he arrived in Seattle, and this was the fifth different brand of coffee he had tried. He remained unimpressed. However, he knew next month Seattle would be invaded by *Buenisimo!*, the best coffee south of the border. It would make his return trip more palatable.

Yet a chance to sample Seattle's famous coffee was hardly the reason Rivera found himself far away from his family. Not that he had a choice. When Mr. Hernandez said, "Go to Seattle," he went. No questions, no protests. Yet *this* job made Rivera sick. He told himself he was a professional and he could do this. It's what he told himself every time that Mr. Hernandez required him to do something distasteful. Rivera hated dipping a rival gang member's hand in acid. Neither did he care for shooting a man's beloved dog just to make a point. But *this* assignment? This one was exceptionally cruel. It was so monstrous in its nature that Rivera wondered if Mr. Hernandez even had a conscience anymore—or a heart. Of course, Rivera could refuse. But he loved his family too much. He preferred ever so slightly this sordid existence over death, even if it was a half-step above. Choosing one over the other was about a 50-50 proposition. Rivera chose to live.

Rivera shook his partner, Juan Morales, who had just dozed off in the passenger's seat.

"It's time. Wake up."

Morales rubbed his face and looked through the rain-speckled windshield at their target meandering down the sidewalk. The pulsing wipers swept away a handful of raindrops, gliding across the glass creating a clean space for more raindrops to gather.

"That's him," Rivera said.

He eased the car forward and stopped about 10 feet past the target.

With great precision and efficiency, Morales jumped out of the car and grabbed the confused boy. Jake resisted his abductor yet was only able to make one muted call for help. Rivera secured the boy's arms and mouth; Morales snatched his legs. The boy squirmed and tried to kick free, but in less than two seconds, he was in the backseat of the Town Car wedged between the seat and Morales' left knee. It was a fight the boy had no chance of winning. His muffled cries went unheard.

Morales grinned and patted Rivera on the back as they pulled away from the curb and headed down the street.

"We got him!" Morales said.

Rivera said nothing. He adjusted the mirror so he could only see Morales. Seeing the terror in the boy's eyes as Morales was wrangling him in the street was too intensely personal for Rivera. With a six-year-old son of his own, Rivera could hardly stomach this task. But he couldn't let this get personal. This was business, a business he had to conduct professionally and efficiently or his own family might end up victims of Mr. Hernandez.

Morales couldn't stop grinning as he basked in his moment of triumph, albeit a sick one—a 28-year-old man overpowering a six-year-old boy 180 pounds his junior. He looked down at his catch, brooding over him with a gruff voice.

"*Hola*, Jakie boy."

CHAPTER 2

CAL MURPHY FINISHED a rare morning meeting with his editor and was taking care of a few last-minute details when Josh Moore approached his desk.

"So, hotshot reporter, are you ready to cover the Super Bowl?" Josh was unable to hide his jealousy with the snarky question.

"It's just the nineteenth game of the season, Josh," Cal answered trying to sound cool and professional. "Just a really over-hyped game."

Cal knew downplaying his exuberance for covering the Super Bowl was the quickest way to end any possible tete-a-tete with his former college roommate. It took Cal just two years to land most sportswriters' dream job. In such a competitive environment, Cal's friends on the sports staff were scarce. Not wanting to push away his best one, Cal dropped the act.

"Look, Josh, I'm super excited about this opportunity—and I really wish you could join me," Cal said. "It would be a lot of fun."

"But then who would be here to write about Seattle Prep and Rainier Beach's big basketball game this weekend?"

Cal shook his head and smiled. Josh had returned to benign sarcasm rather than the harsh ridicule. Their friendship had risen above jealousy, at least for the moment.

"Have a great time. I'll expect lots of great stories from the award-winning Cal Murphy."

Cal smiled and stuffed the last of his files into his computer bag then zipped it shut. He flung the strap across his shoulder and saluted Josh as he began walking down the stairs. It was 8:30 a.m. and he had just enough time to make it to the airport for his 10 a.m. flight. He would also squeeze in a call to Kelly Mendoza.

After the pair of journalists exposed a cover-up in Statenville, Idaho, two years ago, Cal and Kelly had their choice of jobs. Cal chose *The Times* in Seattle. With offers in Seattle as well, Kelly instead opted for a job with the Associated Press bureau in Salt Lake City. Her decision disappointed Cal. He wanted to pursue the romantic inklings that he sensed between them. However, Cal didn't let his heart override his professional ambition. He wanted to cover a team in the NFL and Salt Lake City didn't have one. Besides, Seattle contained all of Cal's favorite boyhood teams, his familiar stomping grounds near the University of Washington, and an awesome music scene. He chose familiarity and opportunity over romance. But he hadn't given up on Kelly yet.

He dialed her number.

"Hey, Cal," came Kelly's familiar voice from the other end. "You in Houston yet?"

"Not yet, but I will be soon. What about you? Are you going?"

"Well, the bureau isn't sending me, if that's what you mean. But I'll be there as a fan. My uncle asked me to go with him. He usually goes with an old war buddy, but he couldn't make it—so I got invited. And he didn't have to ask his favorite niece twice."

"That's great. We'll have to catch up then when I get some free time. When are you leaving?"

"Our flight gets in Tuesday night at 9:30. Want to meet up then?"

"Sure. Call me when you land."

Cal pressed "end" on his iPhone and let his giddiness spread throughout his body. If he and Kelly were just friends, why did he always feel so excited about seeing or talking with her? It was a question he hoped to answer in Houston.

But he couldn't deny the fact that his excitement over this trip was also due to the fact that he was covering his first Super Bowl—with his favorite team playing in it. Even better was his scheduled one-on-one interview with Seattle quarterback Noah Larson the next morning. Sometimes Cal felt like it was all a dream.

* * *

NOAH FINISHED PACKING, threw his bags into his Toyota Tundra and climbed in. The silver 4x4 wasn't what people expected an NFL star to drive, but Noah favored substance over style. His dad used to drill that mantra into his head: "Substance matters more than style, son." Especially after a game where Noah's statistics were abysmal but the team still won. "Real leaders are willing to sacrifice everything for the good of the whole," Noah's dad would say. "Leaders don't want medals or accolades—they just want to help those around them accomplish a common vision. If you remember that, you'll be a great leader."

Eventually, that philosophy sunk in and stuck. And after two state championships and a national title in college, Noah adopted this idea for all parts of his life. However, it made for a challenging life in the NFL, where people judged you by how much you were going to help their fantasy league team. But that was somebody else's fantasy. It was his reality, a reality that was on the verge of being one he only dreamed about as a child—Super Bowl champs.

Noah pulled out of the driveway and onto the quiet street. He was lost in thought reflecting on his NFL career. The windshield wipers provided a soothing rhythmic background to his contemplative mood. He dreamed of playing in the NFL but never realized it would go so well. His hard work had paid off in various accolades and handsome contracts. But now he could earn a payoff on the sport's ultimate stage: The Super Bowl. Now he had a chance to write a fairytale ending—"Noah Larson leads Seahawks to Super Bowl victory and rides off into the sunset."

The ringing of his phone interrupted his pleasant mood. Restricted number. Probably one of his teammates, who all blocked their numbers. Privacy was challenging enough without some wacko fan tweeting your number to the fanbase.

He glanced out the window and saw Jake's soccer ball on the sidewalk. This was curious. Jake loved that ball and would never just leave it laying around, much less abandon it before school. Confused at this discovery, Noah answered the phone.

"Hello?" Noah said, putting his truck in park and starting to get out.

"Is this Noah Larson?" asked the unfamiliar voice on the other end.

Noah stopped. "Yes. Who is this?"

"The *who* is not important, Mr. Larson. What's important is that you do as I say if you ever want to see Jake alive again."

The voice was heavily accented, maybe someone from Latin America somewhere. Noah couldn't be sure.

"What? No. Who is this? ..."

"No, you do the listening. I do the talking. *Comprende?*"

"What do you want? Money? I'll give you whatever you want."

"That's good, Mr. Larson. But I don't want your money. I want you to do something for me—and if you do it, your son will live."

"What do you want me to do?"

"I want you to make sure that the Seahawks lose the Super Bowl by a comfortable margin."

"Are you out of your mind?!" Jake asked. "I can't control that."

"Oh, I think you can, Mr. Larson. A bad decision here. A bad throw there. You can blame it on the pressure of playing in the Super Bowl and no one will be the wiser. Nobody expects much out of you anyway."

For someone who wanted to coerce Noah into helping him, the mystery caller certainly lacked any charm. Yet his persuasion was strong enough—he had taken his son.

"It's very simple, Mr. Larson. You lose by a touchdown or so and your son will be returned to you immediately after the game.

If not, you will never see him again. Understand."

"Yes, I understand."

"And lastly, no authorities either. If you contact them, we will return his body to you in pieces. Otherwise, we look forward to watching the Miami Dolphins beat the Seahawks in the Super Bowl on Sunday."

The line went dead. Noah scooped up Jake's ball and held it close as the sky opened up and dumped a fresh deluge.

CHAPTER 3

RIVERA HIT SEND ON HIS disposable cell phone, removed the battery and threw it out the window. Transmitting a photo of a man's son he took by force was unpleasant, but it had to be done.

He checked his watch. It was 10:30 and they had 30 minutes to reach Boeing Field and prepare Mr. Hernandez's Gulfstream G450 for the flight back to Juarez. They had a schedule to follow, if only for Mr. Hernandez's pleasure. He didn't tolerate tardiness or inefficiency of any kind, yet he never actually fired anyone. He just made sure you never came to work again. It was a major reason his operation ran so smoothly. The examples made of a few served as sufficient motivation for the other employees.

Rivera glanced in his rearview mirror. Jake was slumped in the back right corner, duck tape over his mouth. Rivera thought the tape was unnecessary but Morales insisted. It was Mr. Hernandez's orders, and a wise directive. One empathetic employee and the plan would disintegrate—and Mr. Hernandez had too much riding on this job to have any missteps. Jake stared listlessly out the window as they neared the airfield.

Airport security personnel were paid to look the other way at any destination Mr. Hernandez's planes flew to. And while Seattle was not a regular route, three of the guards were paid handsomely for those occasional visits.

In secret Rivera hoped it would be a different guard, one who might want to fully inspect the vehicle and politely decline any bribes. But it wasn't. The security guard didn't even glimpse at Rivera as he waved him through to Mr. Hernandez's hangar.

In thirty minutes, Rivera would fly out of the city, leaving behind its bitter coffee, its dreary weather, and his darkest sin.

* * *

NOAH GASPED FOR AIR. How could this be happening? How could anyone take Jake? What kind of monster would do that to a six-year-old boy—*his* boy?

He calmed down, returned to his truck and began driving toward the airport. The rain hardly concerned him any more, neither did the Super Bowl. He only wanted his son back.

He had to think. What was the best course of action? He had to put aside his desire for vengeance. Its value was far less than Jake's life. Revenge was something he couldn't think about. But he felt helpless. He couldn't feign an illness or an injury for fear of losing Jake. He needed outside help. But first, he needed to call Ellen.

He dialed her number on his cell phone.

"Hey. You at the airport yet?"

Noah couldn't think of a gentle way to break it to Ellen. "It's horrible, Ellen. I found Jake's soccer ball. These men called me and said they had Jake. Said they would kill him if I didn't lose the game."

"Wait, slow down. What are you saying?"

"Jake's been kidnapped."

Ellen went silent for a moment. Then came a fury of questions, screaming and sobbing. Noah could barely answer Ellen as he struggled to fight back his own tears. Eventually, he broke down, too, and couldn't tell whether the drops in his field of vision were raindrops or tears.

Finally, Ellen composed herself and asked the most important question, the one question that needed to be answered.

"So, what are we going to do?" she asked.

"Well, the only thing I can do—fly to Houston and make sure we lose the Super Bowl."

CHAPTER 4

CAL TURNED OFF HIS eReader per the flight attendant's instructions. United flight 1186 would touch down at George Bush International Airport in twenty minutes. Flying never really bothered Cal. But the landing part did. He became nervous.

Without anything to occupy his mind, Cal resorted to good old-fashioned print. Printed words on a paper—it was integral to how he earned his living. But he preferred anything that glowed. Right now, he just wanted anything to look at other than an emergency landing instruction placard. He reached for the bulging pack of magazines in the seat pocket in front of him. *Hemispheres,* United's magazine full of articles and beautiful photographs of destinations the airline flew to. *Sky Mall,* a catalog for those who just couldn't wait to purchase an overpriced dog orthopedic "comfy" couch for $250 while soaring over the Grand Canyon. And *Time.*

Cal opted for *Time.* Without even glancing at its contents, he knew *Time* would contain at least some semblance of journalism, articles written without the express purpose of coercing him to open up his wallet for something he didn't want or need. Then Cal looked at the cover. He was instantly hooked.

The title, "Is God Really Good?", was plastered over a collage of images that comprised the worst of this world—starving children in Africa, guns and missiles, disease, murder, destruction. Cal thought it was an interesting question from *Time*, especially considering its infamous "Is God Dead?" cover from 1966. Cal chuckled at how *Time* had now become now sure of God's existence, but just suspect of his actions.

Cal dove into the article, exploring the dichotomy between the best and worst of the human race. But the author kept bringing the story back to that one question that irked Cal: If God is so good, why do bad things happen to good people? Cal read for another ten minutes but the article went nowhere in its conclusion. There was no strong voice—just statements that conjured up more questions. It left Cal just as frustrated with the thesis question as before he started reading the article. He closed the magazine and slid it back into the seat pocket and sat upright.

The flight attendant's final instructions in preparation for landing came over the intercom and Cal tightened his seat belt. He looked out his window at the bustling Houston freeway as the plane made its final approach at George Bush International Airport.

He groaned. The planes' wheels touched down a shade after 4:30 p.m. and he knew what he had ahead of him; it wasn't exciting. Fighting grumpy travelers. Wrestling his bag off the carousel, if it even made it. Picking up his rental car and merging into gridlock on Highway 59, heading for an even bigger gridlock downtown. Then he would stand in line behind a bunch of underpaid hacks, pretentious sportscasters, and former NFL stars to check in at the Four Seasons. The least glamorous part of his job was about to commence.

Due to a regular season game against the Houston Texans just a few months before, Cal was somewhat familiar with the airport. Every possible concourse remained under construction just as it was during his last visit. Wires dangled from the ceiling. Unfinished sheet rock held temporary signage to direct travelers. The smell of sawdust hung in the air. Cal thought it might make a perfect backdrop for a horror movie if the place was deserted. But it wasn't. It was bustling with travelers coming and going, talking or checking email on their smart phones. Everyone seemed engrossed with their little world.

But Cal watched closely, inspecting as many details about as many people as he could. It was a game he used to play with his dad whenever they went out in public. They identified someone and had to gather three pieces of information about that person with just two questions. It was called "Three Things." With only two questions to gather three pieces of information, you either had to be clever with your questions or extra observant. Usually the person was the clerk checking them out at the grocery store. And the information was benign. Married or single? Original hair color or dyed? Left-handed or right-handed? Nothing earth shattering. But it taught Cal to look for details, the kind of details that make an award-winning investigative reporter, even if those details pertained to the sports world.

Cal followed the masses toward baggage claim and played "Three Things" by himself. He identified two businessmen cheating on their wives while they strolled through the airport with their girlfriends. He also noticed three players' wives, which wasn't so tough to do. Lots of fur, five-inch stilettos, a giant rock on the ring finger, and an unnatural figure. There was even a fluffy little dog, stuffed inside a small carrier and yapping away. However, it was the trailing young nanny with two elementary-aged sons playing hand-held video game devices that were the real giveaways. Cal met plenty of the players' wives during his job covering the Seahawks; they definitely weren't his type. He wanted a down-to-earth woman, a woman who wasn't afraid to set out on the open road in search of adventure, or a good story.

Before he knew it, Cal was thinking about Kelly. He would see her tomorrow night. She was exactly the kind of woman he had in mind ... his type. Not even someone just like her. Just her.

Cal's phone began to buzz, jolting him back to reality. It was the office, calling to make sure he had arrived safely and would still be able to file a short story later that evening.

He hung up his phone and suspended his game. He was in Houston covering the Super Bowl. And his childhood favorite team, no less. But he had to collect his thoughts and focus on his next work task—preparing for his exclusive interview in the morning with Seattle quarterback Noah Larson.

* * *

ON THE SOUTH SIDE of Houston, Noah Larson and the rest of the Seattle Seahawks touched down at Hobby Airport. Charter flights sufficed for most trips, but not this week. For the Super Bowl, Seahawks' owner, Paul Allen, employed one of his two luxury 757s for the team.

Flying into Hobby meant a shorter commute to downtown and less of a traffic headache at this time of day. Of course, charter buses with a state patrol escort to the Four Seasons meant that it didn't really matter where the team landed; they were going to reach their destination more quickly than any regular Joe behind the wheel for his Monday afternoon commute.

But Noah wasn't thinking about any of this. All he could think about was Jake—and Ellen. The news that his son had been kidnapped and was being held ransom for a guaranteed loss in the Super Bowl was only five hours old, yet somehow every second Noah thought about it, it all felt fresh again. Too fresh. Like picking a scab every day and exposing that wound to the elements all over again.

As the team filed off the plane, many of the players looked Noah in the eye and mentioned how unbelievable this experience was— and how it could only be topped by winning the game. They all believed in Noah. Ricky Johnson, Telvin Hayes, Brandon Gomez, Pat Ott. Every single player on the roster believed that Noah was going to lead the team to victory. Which is why Noah felt phony. As one of the more authentic players in the Seattle locker room, it would be a crippling burden for Noah to keep this secret. He was going to let this entire team down—and there was nothing he could do about it. He wasn't going to lead the Seahawks to victory; he was going to make sure they lost. And lost big.

* * *

THE OASIS WAS FAR from the most impressive casino resorts in Vegas, but it wasn't low class either. Checkered marble floors seemed to sprawl endlessly from one section of the casino to the other. Lights flickered on row after row of slot machines. Computer blackjack machines called out to gamblers like the Sirens' song. Listless gamblers sat transfixed while the machine in front of them took their life and their money. Only the craps tables and the sports book had lively human interaction.

Gil Jackson's fingers itched as he walked into The Oasis with a briefcase full of money. More cash than he had ever seen in his life. It was certainly more than he would ever make in his lifetime. For a fleeting moment, Jackson contemplated just walking out the door and heading to the Cayman Islands with all that money. Only the thought of Maria kept him from doing so; that and the two bulky men following him. He found a casino rep and announced his intentions to open an account with the casino, his hands trembling as he went over the details with the man. The amount of the deposit would earn him VIP treatment.

Jackson shook hands with the rep and wound his way through the expansive casino to the sports book. He had to make a bet, a very specific bet.

"I'd like to place a bet for two million dollars on the Dolphins to win," Jackson said.

Jackson collected his betting slip and walked into the cool Las Vegas night. His job was done. He would collect $50,000 for his troubles upon delivering the betting slip to the drop. Just like they said. An easy fifty grand.

* * *

RICKY LONGSHORE PICKED UP the phone and began punching the numbers. He ran the sports book at The Oasis and something didn't seem quite right about Gil Jackson's enormous bet. Not that people didn't bet ridiculous amounts of money on things that would never happen. But Longshore knew *those* people. This latest bet was from a nobody, the proprietor of a sports card collectible store called Mint Condition. In less than 10 minutes, he had called four other sports books to inquire if Mr. Jackson had an account with them. Longshore had to know if this guy was legit. After working in Vegas for 35 years, he knew when something seemed suspect. And Gil Jackson set off alarm bells in his head.

He picked up the phone and made a call.

"This is Anderson."

"Anderson. Longshore here."

"Longshore, what's happening? You guys busy this week ?"

Longshore wasn't in a joking mood.

"More than you know – and that's actually why I called."

"Oh, what's going on?"

"I think we may have a problem in Houston. A big problem."

CHAPTER 5

IT HAD BEEN A LONG NIGHT and a new day was dawning. Rivera had stayed awake as much as he could with his wide-eyed hostage. He wanted to make sure Jake didn't freak out or become a pain to watch. He knew what might happen if he did. This was about controlling the situation, making sure it was peaceful.

But that wasn't an easy task in this environment. Dirty concrete floor. A leaky roof. Hay strewn about the floor. A rusted frame for a single bed. And a black and white TV with an antennae. The walls looked like they might fall down with any significant attempt to knock them over. It was enough to put anyone on edge. But despite the surroundings, Rivera did his best with what he did have: conversation. He brought up numerous topics he thought might bring Jake out of his shocked state: video games, football, school, future dreams. Nothing worked all that well. Jake muttered one- or two-word answers, if anything. Rivera knew the boy was an emotional mess and Morales was about to make it worse.

Rivera didn't want to tie Jake's feet together; they looked about the same size as his son Juan's feet. He didn't want to tie Jake's hands together either. But he tied them both. This kid wasn't going anywhere, but Rivera knew it was best to heed instruction. Mr. Hernandez's compound was no place for compassion. Not even a moment of kindness could inch through the door. Mr.

Hernandez was always watching.

"When am I going to see my mom and dad again?" Jake finally asked.

"Hopefully soon," Rivera said.

Rivera finished tying the last knot and swung Jake's feet onto the bed so his prisoner could relax a bit. Jake's initial terror had worn off and he felt comfortable with Rivera. Then Morales entered the room, storming in with a bottle of tequila in one hand and a Glock 19 in the other. He sneered at Jake before crashing on top of a wooden folding chair near Jake's bed. It was far too early to be drinking, but Morales' love affair with alcohol was nothing he tried to hide. Rivera worried something bad could happen to Jake if he left him alone with Morales. But it was time for a shift change, another directive from Mr. Hernandez that could not be usurped. However, Rivera felt obliged to give Morales a fair warning about his behavior.

"What are you doing?" Rivera said in a hushed voice. "It's not a good idea to be drinking like this, especially in front of the kid."

Morales bristled at the rebuke.

"Who are you to tell me what to do?" Morales roared. "If I want to smack this little kid around, I will."

And with his bold statement, Morales backhanded Jake, catching him just below his right cheekbone. Jake's entire body lurched toward the wall and only stopped when Jake's head smacked it hard. He started crying as a wave of terror washed over his face. Rivera thought Jake was begging him to stay with his eyes. But those sad eyes reminded Rivera that he had his own family waiting for him at home—and he didn't need to waste any more time here.

"Go easy on the kid," Rivera said. As he left the room and walked down the hall, Rivera heard another sound of a head slapping up against the wooden wall. He cringed ... and hoped Jake would still be alive when he returned later that evening.

CHAPTER 6

CAL'S ALARM BUZZED, and he rolled over to look at the clock. Six a.m. It was too early for the sun to be up, much less Cal. It was the worst thing about traveling east while living on the west coast. Hours of sleep were lost that could never be regained. At least, not if you believed in Murphy's law of sleep deprivation: if you lose an hour of sleep, it's gone forever. He told everyone about his rule, even though it was ridiculous. He figured he could get away with such a corny joke since his last name was indeed Murphy. He even invented a story to tell about Captain Ed Murphy, his great uncle. It always garnered a good laugh from his audience.

It felt like four a.m. to Cal. But on this Tuesday morning, he figured it was well worth losing both hours. He had an exclusive interview with Noah Larson before the circus that's called Super Bowl Media Day commenced. Answering the bastion of goofy questions by TV personalities and comedians masquerading as journalists was enough to turn anyone's brain to mush. But Cal was going to get Noah at his finest; at least that's what Cal had heard.

Among NFL circles, Noah was renowned for his diligent work ethic, a regimen that started at 5 a.m. each day. He studied game film like there was going to be a comprehensive test about it later that afternoon. He would fill up half a yellow legal pad during a film session, dissecting his opponents' weaknesses and strengths. And he would do it all without one drop of coffee. Noah hated the side effects of coffee.

Yet when Cal wandered down to the Four Seasons restaurant at 7 a.m., he saw Noah sitting alone at a table, cradling a cup of coffee. Cal wondered if his sources were accurate. Noah seemed to be lost in thought as he stared blankly at the table. The who's-who in the NFL sat at tables surrounding Noah and all were too lost in their conversations to notice the star quarterback. Cal thought it was a surreal scene.

"Good morning, Noah," Cal said, offering his hand to shake.

"Morning, Cal," Noah mumbled, ignoring Cal's hand.

"How are you feeling about the game on Sunday?"

"Good."

Noah's terse answer took Cal by surprise. After covering the Seahawks all season, Cal felt he had developed a good rapport with the quarterback. They had exchanged stories of playing football when they were kids. They traded restaurant recommendations when out of town for a game, and shared their favorite spots in the Pacific Northwest to get away from the hustle and bustle of life in the big city. But to Cal, that suddenly felt like a distant memory. *What was wrong with Noah?*

Cal pulled out his recorder and his notebook with questions for Noah. Small talk was apparently not in order today.

"So, Noah, as a veteran quarterback in this league who has never made it to the Super Bowl, what does this post-season experience mean to you ... to finally make it to this game?"

"Getting here is a big deal, but nobody remembers you if you lose. We still have some unfinished business."

Score one for the clichéd response. Noah usually offered a more original quote, but Cal realized he was in for a fight to pry something out of the unusually grumpy quarterback.

"What do you think was different about this season, compared to year's past, that enabled you to get to this point?"

Noah stared at his cup for a quiet moment before answering. "We played better as a team. The front office made some great moves and helped us shore up a few weak areas. And if truth be told, we got a few lucky breaks in the NFC championship game."

Noah's admission of luck referred to a play that set the sports world buzzing. In Seattle's upset win over Super Bowl favorite San Francisco, Noah's touchdown pass was a highlight for the ages. With Seattle trailing by four points with less than 30 seconds remaining, Noah threw a pass that was tipped by a defender and deflected into the waiting arms of his favorite wide receiver Telvin Hayes, who raced into the end zone for the game-winning score. Instead of being the goat by throwing an interception, Noah escaped a hero. SportsCenter replayed the catch ad nauseum. Sports writers dubbed the play, "The Immaculate Reception II."

Cal continued with his pre-determined line of questioning. He asked Noah about his favorite Super Bowl, if he was approaching this game any differently, and if he felt extra pressure to since Seattle was favored heavily to win.

Noah answered the questions, but he appeared distant to Cal. The responses were bland, even canned—far from the originality Cal expected out of Noah.

"Excuse me, Cal. I need some more coffee." Noah had drained the pitcher on the table and went in search of a server for a fresh one.

Cal began flipping the pages in his notebook, wondering how he was going to turn this lifeless interview into the compelling article his editors expected.

Then Noah's phone buzzed. A new message appeared on the screen along with a small picture.

Normally, Cal would ignore the phone out of respect for the quarterback's privacy. But he couldn't, not with the picture that flashed in front of his eyes and the threatening message that accompanied it.

Noah returned to the table with a fresh pitcher.

"What else you got for me, Cal?" Noah asked as he sat down.

"Well, I didn't have this one written down and it's personal."

"Go ahead."

"Is everything OK, Noah?"

"What do you mean?"

"I mean, is there something you want to tell me but can't?"

Noah began to shift in his chair. He avoided eye contact with Cal. Then his phone's screen flashed on, reminding him of the unread message. He snatched the phone and shoved it into his pocket.

"I promise I wasn't being nosy, Noah, but I saw the message and that picture. I can't ignore it."

Noah grabbed Cal's recorder and turned it off.

"You have to, Cal!" Noah pleaded in a hushed whisper. "They said if I told anyone they would kill my son."

"When did this happen?" Cal asked.

"Look, I can't tell you anything. Just pretend like you didn't see it."

"I can't, Noah. Do you realize what you're asking me to do?"

"It's for my son, Cal! If I don't do what they ask, he's going to die! Do you want his blood on your hands? Do you know what that would do to my wife?"

"I've got a friend at the FBI. He can help."

"No, Cal. I've just got to handle this on my own."

"Noah, you can't throw the game."

"After the way we got here, I don't think it will surprise anyone if I make a few poor throws that cost our team a couple of touchdowns."

"I have to report on this."

"You have no proof and your editor will never allow it. Cal, please, I'm begging you. I'll make it worth your while to keep quiet."

"Are you trying to bribe me?"

"My son's life depends on me losing this game. Wouldn't you do the same if you were me?"

"I don't want your money, Noah. But I'll think about holding this. Does anyone else know?"

"Only Ellen. Please, Cal. Please don't say anything to anyone."

"OK, Noah. I'll think about it. I understand the situation you're in, but this is wrong. You should let some people help you get your son back before the game."

"I can't take that risk, Cal. Thanks for trying to understand."

"All right. I'll see you at media day. Take care, and I'm sorry someone is doing this awful thing to you."

"Thanks."

Cal gathered his pen and pad as Noah slid the recorder across the table. He got up and left Noah alone again. Pondering the dramatic information he had just learned, Cal walked back to his hotel room.

It all made sense now. Noah's depressed demeanor as well as his caffeine binge. The terse responses. Who wouldn't react like that?

Rumors swirled all season long that Noah would retire at season's end. And here he was, poised to go out on top and cap his career with a Super Bowl victory. It would have been a storybook ending. Instead, it was every dad's worst nightmare, a true horror story in the making.

Cal held information to what would undoubtedly be one of the biggest sports stories of his life. But he would have to betray Noah's trust to write it. It would forever tarnish the reputation of one of the most well-liked quarterbacks in the league; or worse, cost Jake his life. Was any story worth that? Suddenly, Cal wished he was covering a high school basketball game in Seattle rather than wrestling over such a huge decision. He needed more time to mull over what to do.

* * *

NOAH RE-READ THE MESSAGE on his phone and stared at the chilling photo of Jake. His son didn't appear to have any bruises on him, but maybe the gag was covering them up. Either way, the image haunted Noah. This wasn't a bad dream. This was life at its worst.

"Lose by a touchdown if you want to see your son alive again."

The message mocked him. His chance at finishing his career as a Super Bowl champion derailed by some random lowlifes trying to make some money. Noah wondered how he could get through the day without breaking down. How could he face the media and pretend like he was serious about trying to win? It would require his best acting job, something he wasn't good at anyway. His scant commercial endorsements proved this fact.

But he would have to manage. He had no choice.

CHAPTER 7

CAL BEGAN POUNDING OUT THE OUTLINE of his story on Noah, leaving some spaces to fill in the predictable quotes his teammates would make about him. In a couple of hours, reporters from all over the world would descend upon Reliant Stadium to try and get a newsworthy comment or reaction from a player. To Cal, it was a reminder of all things that were wrong with journalism, if you could even call it that. At least ten reporters would try to upstage the players with some ridiculous stunt or line of questioning. Cal wanted no part of it, but it was required for finishing his extensive feature story on Seattle's beloved quarterback.

Cal's phone buzzed. It was one of his college fraternity brothers, Jarrett Anderson.

"Agent Anderson, to what do I owe this great honor?" Cal said.

"Well, I have a fellow agent in Miami who wants to place a little wager on the game and I thought I would check with the expert first on whether it was safe for me to do that."

Cal laughed nervously. "It's going to be a good one."

"Seriously?" Anderson asked. "I thought Seattle was supposed to blow them out."

"It could happen but you just never know."

Anderson paused.

"Actually, Cal. That's not the real reason I called. I really wish it was, believe me. But we've got a serious situation here and I was wondering if you've heard anything about rumors of a fix being on."

Cal didn't say a word.

"Cal? Are you there?"

"Yeah, I'm here. What kind of fix are you talking about?"

"I'm talking about someone fixing Sunday's game. We've received a few reports of suspicious betting activity going on from some of the sports books and I thought you might have heard something."

"Heard something? Like what?"

"You know, a player or coach trying to throw the game. Something of that nature."

"No, I don't think I've heard anything like that." Cal was a terrible liar.

"Cal, are you sure? You're acting kind of funny and vague here. This is me. Jarrett. If you've heard something I need to know."

Cal paused. He could ponder all the scenarios of telling Anderson and the likely outcomes for 20 years and never be sure of the right thing. But he had already concluded that Noah was naïve if he thought he would see his son alive again, regardless of what he did. So Cal relied on his instincts.

"OK, look. If I tell you this, you've got to promise to help this guy."

"I'm not making any promises, Cal."

"Well, it's complicated and if you don't promise to help, I don't feel right about divulging this information."

"All right. I'll do my best to help if I can. Just tell me what you know."

"Someone has kidnapped Noah Larson's son, Jake. The ransom is that he has to ensure that Seattle loses or else they're going to kill the boy."

Anderson let out a string of expletives.

"What kind of animal would do such a thing?"

"Don't you deal with people like this every day?"

"Sure, but a little kid? Come on! We're gonna find this guy and string him up."

"Let me know what I can do to help."

"For starters, tell Noah we need to speak with him."

"I'll see what I can do. He's going to hate me though because I told you."

"You can tell him that we do have a lead on a sports memorabilia shop owner. And trust me. He's going to thank you by the time this is all over."

"OK, I'll pass that along and give him your cell number. I'll be in touch."

"Thanks, Cal. Don't worry. We'll find this monster wherever he is."

* * *

RIVERA LOOKED AT JAKE with pity. The innocent kid stuck in the middle of a despicable money grab.

Jake sat on the bed reading through some of the comic books given to him as a way to assuage his boredom.

Rivera could see the fear in the boy's eyes. And who could blame him? Two strange men forcibly took him and put him on an airplane, flying him to some unknown location. He probably wondered why he was there and not getting ready for recess.

"You like Spiderman?" Rivera muttered in his best English.

"Yeah, he's all right," Jake answered. "I like Batman better."

"How come?"

"Because Batman doesn't have any super powers. He just beats up the bad guys and saves everyone. He's a real hero."

"I like Batman, too."

"Well, Batman wouldn't like you. He'd beat you up if he were here."

Rivera said nothing. He didn't like being called a bad guy. He wasn't bad; he was good. He just worked for a bad man.

"Look, Jake. I have a son too, and I know he would be scared if something like this happened to him."

"I'm not scared."

"It's OK to be scared. But don't worry. I'm not going to hurt you."

"That's what that other guy said before he hit me."

"I'm not like that guy."

"You're helping him out, aren't you?"

"Yes, but …" Rivera knew a nuanced response would not work with a kid, so he stopped. "Look, I want to help you."

"Then take me back to my dad."

"I can't right now, but I will. I promise."

Jake eyed Rivera closely before turning his attention back to his comic book in silence.

Rivera knew Jake was an innocent victim of circumstance. He felt the same way, too.

CHAPTER 8

JUST AFTER 10 a.m., Cal headed downstairs for Media Day. Reporters jammed into every available space on one of six charter buses destined for Reliant Stadium. The scene entertained Cal more than any Super Bowl ever could. Veteran sports writers engaged in a game of one-upmanship. Television reporters bragging about the hottest celebrity's party they attended. Cameramen boasting about their clients. Photographers detailing how they landed their latest magazine cover shot. The egos contained in this 45-foot metal box would have given Freud a lifetime of research.

Cal enjoyed listening to the banter for a few moments. But he snapped back to the reality once he saw a missing child billboard anchored along the side of Highway 59. How would Noah react when he told him? What would he say? Would Noah instruct other players to not grant him any interviews? It would be out of character for Noah to get enraged, especially publicly. But this situation would test anyone.

Though it was Cal's first Super Bowl, Media Day was exactly how he envisioned it: a 50-ring circus without the animals. Everywhere he looked there was a Seahawk player being swarmed by media members. Even the punter, Patt Ott, was worth five reporters and a cameraman.

One woman even parachuted in wearing nothing but a bikini and a helmet with a camera attached to it. Security personnel quickly descended upon her to remove her from the stadium before she flashed her credentials. Cal could only guess what her story angle would be—herself.

If only that was the craziest moment of Media Day. But it wasn't. Some reporter brought his accordion and tried to get players to sing a ridiculous polka song he had written about the Super Bowl. His gag was received about as well as replacement officials. Other reporters lustily booed his act when he interrupted their serious interviews, effectively ruining the shtick.

There were plenty of reporters on hand trying to be serious about their jobs. They asked pertinent questions about the season, the game, the opponents. It was refreshing. But any rapport building between a small crowd of reporters and the player disintegrated when a knucklehead would ask them if they'd ever done it on the 50-yard line or which lineman could drink the most beer in one sitting.

Despite the chaotic scene, Cal managed to locate Telvin Hayes and get a few quiet moments with him to discuss the Seahawks' quarterback. Hayes put his big ego aside when talking about Noah. Maybe it was because he was a veteran, but Noah had the respect of every player on the team—even the unlikely candidates such as Hayes. Even though Hayes' miracle catch was a result of his own physical ability and a fortuitous tip, he refused to say anything negative about Noah's pass.

Ricky Johnson, Seattle's leading rusher, handled Cal's interview the same way. Nothing but class in his responses about the team's undisputed leader.

"How do you feel about your chances Sunday?" Cal asked.

"With Noah at quarterback, you know we're going to have a chance to win the game," Johnson said. "He has an amazing ability to take this team on his back and carry it when necessary. There's not a guy in our locker room who wouldn't trust him with his life."

Cal scribbled down a few more answers on his notepad before turning off his recorder and scanning the field for Noah. Dark clouds gathered overhead, replacing the bright sunshine. The stadium lights began flickering on. There were only five more minutes left before Seattle players yielded the field to Miami's. Where was Noah?

Cal suddenly lurched forward as someone hit him square in the back. Accident or on purpose? Cal couldn't tell, but it sent him flailing a few yards down the field.

"Oh, hey, Cal." said the familiar voice. "Sorry about that."

Cal spun to see Associated Press sports writer Damon James standing behind him.

"No worries," Cal said.

"You know those pushy cameramen, gotta get the shot of that latest faux reporter trying to upstage the real celebrities," James said, referring to the reason for bumping into Cal in the first place. "So, how are you?"

"Oh, you know how it is. Same old, same old," Cal replied.

"Well, I saw you this morning ... and getting an exclusive with the Seahawks' quarterback a few days before the Super Bowl isn't exactly 'same old, same old.' "

"True. I've got a good relationship with Noah. He was nice enough to do an exclusive," Cal said, playing coy as he kept scanning the crowd for that same quarterback.

"You keep this up, Cal, and you'll be dragging one of those cameramen around with ESPN."

"I doubt that," Cal said.

"Well, keep it up. Good to see you. I gotta run."

"OK. See ya, Damon." Cal nodded and watched the writer walk off before continuing his search for Noah Larson.

In the east corner of the end zone, he saw a large crowd of reporters begin to disperse around Seattle's star quarterback. A Seahawks media relations personnel motioned that the interview was over and begin ushering the reporters toward the center of the field. Cal hustled toward Noah, fighting the stream of reporters, most of them unwilling to cede any space to Cal.

"Noah!" Cal called.

Noah turned around.

"I'm sorry. He's done for the day," the Seahawks' employee said.

"No, it's all right. I'll talk to him for a minute," Noah said. He motioned for privacy from his handler.

"Are you going to stay quiet about this, Cal?" Noah asked quietly.

"Look, Noah, the FBI called me, and ..."

Noah didn't let him finish.

"You didn't tell them, did you?"

"I had no choice. They know the game is being fixed and asked if I knew anything. I couldn't lie to them."

"I trusted you, Cal!" Noah said, raising his voice. "You told me you wouldn't say anything!"

"I said I'd consider it, but I didn't have a choice."

The commotion in the end zone suddenly became a focal point for all the media. By the time the cameras began rolling, Noah held a handful of Cal's shirt with his fist.

"If they kill my son, I'm holding you responsible," Noah whispered.

"Look, the FBI wants to help you. They're not going to let your son die. They need to talk to you to find out who took him. They'll get him back."

"You don't know that," Noah said, releasing Cal's shirt and pushing him away.

"I know my friend Agent Anderson is working the case, and he promised me he would do all that he could. Please call him."

Cal felt the cameras burning a hole in him by this point. He discreetly put a card with Anderson's number on it into Noah's hand. "They've got a lead on a guy placing wild bets in Vegas. But they need more information from you. Do the right thing, Noah. They'll help get your son back."

Noah took the card and stormed off.

Cal sighed and looked down at the freshly painted grass. He felt like the dirt beneath it. Rain began pelting him. He looked up and saw the media members scattering across the stadium in search of cover. He slid his notepad and recorder into his bag and walked off the field.

Cal didn't desire to stick around for interviews with any of the Dolphins players. He especially didn't want to hear Miami quarterback Hunter Newton drone on about his heroics in the AFC championship game. Everyone knew the Dolphins were in the Super Bowl because of their defense, not their quarterback. Newton grated on Cal like nobody else. Maybe it was the fact that he was a media darling while playing on a traditional powerhouse college team from the South—and that his success was always due to someone else, like his Heisman Trophy running back. Or maybe it was because he never praised his teammates. But Cal never liked him. Hunter's father even asked colleges to pay a large sum of money for his son's services. The NCAA investigated and they never found enough evidence, but anyone with half a brain knew they were guilty. And while he was an athletic player, Hunter was a living, breathing Me-Monster and Cal despised him.

But Cal didn't need to stay behind, not today. *The Times'* lead columnist was focusing on the Dolphins, releasing Cal from writing mundane stories that didn't interest Seattle readers. Cal found a media charter bus and returned to the hotel with a small group of reporters. The rain streaming down the bus windows blurred the view of the Houston skyline. Cal disappeared into his thoughts.

Did he do the right thing? Did he lose Noah's trust forever? Would his decision cost Jake his life?

He needed to talk with someone about what was happening. He needed Kelly.

CHAPTER 9

BY THE TIME CAL RETURNED to his room, his phone buzzed. It was his editor, Thurston Fink.

"Hey, Fink. What's happening?"

"Cal, you're supposed to report the news, not make it!" Fink shouted.

The vague reprimand caught Cal off guard.

"What are you talking about, Fink?"

"I'm talking about your altercation with Larson. There's video of you two going at it on several websites already."

"What? We were just having a conversation."

"Well, it looks like he's about to rip your head off. The star quarterback of the Seahawks in a tussle with a reporter? That will even beat bikini babes on Super Bowl Media Day."

"Look, Fink, I can explain."

"You better start talking fast. You know I don't put up with that garbage on my staff. It's a privilege to work here, not some right."

"I know, I know. It was a misunderstanding."

"Was it? Or is there something else I should know about?"

"Why do you say that?"

"Earlier today, I got a call from an FBI agent asking about any rumors we might have heard regarding a member of the Seahawks planning on throwing the game Sunday. Heard anything like that?"

It was one thing to lie to the FBI. It was worse to lie to Fink. The hardened sports editor was good at his job, if not the best in the business. But he didn't get that way by coddling his reporters. Nor did he take any crap from them. If you didn't tell him every fact you knew when he asked you, he would explain the facts of his position: The best sports writers in the world begged to work for him, and if you didn't respect him enough to tell him the truth, he would find someone who would.

"So, this morning, I had my exclusive with Noah over breakfast. When he got up to get another pot of coffee, a text message and photo appeared on his phone."

"Wait, Noah was drinking coffee?" Fink never missed a detail.

"Yeah, I know, crazy, right? Anyway the photo was a picture of his son with a gag in his mouth along with a threatening message. Fink, someone kidnapped Noah's son, Jake, and if Noah doesn't lose the game, they're going to kill his son."

"No way! This is unbelievable!"

"I'm dead serious, Fink."

"So, what happened today at Media Day?"

"Well, I had told Noah I would think about not telling anyone and if I did, I would let him know beforehand. But before Media Day, a friend of mine from the FBI office in Vegas called me and said they were getting reports of some suspicious bets placed by local sports books and wanted to know if I knew anything. So, I told them what I learned from Noah."

"And Noah wasn't happy, was he?"

"No, he wasn't. And I understand his position. I would probably be mad, too. But I feel like the FBI is the only one who can help him. He's not going to think rationally in a situation like this."

"Does anyone else know?"

"About the kidnapping?"

"The FBI knows now but no other media does, if that's what you mean."

"OK, just file your feature story on Noah for now. We can sit on this if nobody else is going to run it. I'll do that out of respect for Noah. But if anybody else gets wind of this, you know it will be a race to report it. Just keep quiet about it. Got it?"

"Got it."

"Call me after you send us your story."

Cal hung up and felt somewhat relieved. At least Fink knew he wasn't monkeying around with his assignment and losing credibility with the players for some amateurish reporting. Though Fink didn't say it, Cal sensed a tinge of empathy out of his boss. It wasn't much, but it was more than Cal expected from his mentor.

He turned on the television and immediately saw himself in what looked like a heated exchange with Noah. Who was he kidding? It *was* heated.

The suit reporting this bit of "news" from Media Day speculated what the exchange was about with a title stripped beneath the video: "Larson Invades Murph's Turf."

The parachuting bikini babe followed his story. Cal found some humor in the moment and then reminded himself how grateful he was not to work in that part of the journalism industry.

* * *

AFTER CAL FINISHED WRITING his story that afternoon, he lay down to take a short nap. He needed to rest. Parties with required schmoozing filled Cal's social calendar later that evening. He wasn't asleep more than five minutes before his phone rang. It was Kelly.

"Hey, Cal. Whatcha doin'?"

"Well, I was trying to take a nap, but you ruined that idea."

Kelly laughed.

"Good to see you're working hard during Super Bowl week. But I thought you might be prepping for some radio talk show appearances after your little spat with Larson."

"Look, it's not what it seems."

"Oh, really? It looked like he was ready to spike you in the end zone there from the footage I saw."

"Ah, television. They can edit anything to make it appear juicier than it was."

"Well, what were you talking about then?"

"I'm not sure I can talk about it, to be honest." Cal needed to change the subject fast before Kelly got too curious. "You still up for getting together tonight?"

"Sure thing. I'll call you after I get checked in at the hotel."

"Sounds good. Talk to you then."

Cal hung up and turned his phone off. He needed some uninterrupted peace.

CHAPTER 10

GIL JACKSON DRUMMED HIS FINGERS on the glass case holding his prized mint-condition merchandise inside his sports memorabilia store. A signed Honus Wagner baseball card. A soccer ball signed by New York Cosmos' international stars Pelé, Giorgio Chinaglia, and Franz Beckenbauer. A football signed by Walter Payton from Super Bowl XX. But these were essentially worthless to him until a customer paid his asking price.

When the economy boomed, no fan thought twice about dropping $500 for a signed card of his favorite player. But a market bomb replaced the boom. Jackson felt fortunate to garner $500 in sales in a day.

Difficult times made it easy to say yes to a simple proposal: Place a large bet at a local casino and collect $50,000. Jackson only made half that in the past year through his business. When one of his regular customers, Diego, made the offer to Jackson, he didn't have to ask twice.

It was five minutes before noon, five minutes before Diego gave Jackson $50,000 for three betting slips.

Jackson stopped drumming when a black sedan stopped along the curb outside his shop and two men in suits stepped out of the car. They headed straight for his front door.

"Mr. Jackson?" one of the men asked.

"Yes, I'm Gil Jackson."

"We need to speak with you."

"Look, now isn't a good time. Who are you?"

"I'm federal agent Jarrett Anderson with the FBI and this is my colleague Sid Gant. We have a few questions for you regarding a case we're investigating."

"Can you come back later?"

"How about six o'clock at your house tonight?"

"OK, sounds good. You know where I live?"

Anderson smiled. "We know where everyone lives."

Jackson forced a chuckle. "OK, see you then."

* * *

JACKSON'S MIND BEGAN TO RACE once the agents left the store. *What could they want?* He hadn't done anything wrong in placing those bets. *It has to be about Carlita.* She was in the U.S. illegally. They weren't married yet, but they were engaged. He couldn't imagine life without her. *The feds couldn't send her home, could they?*

Before Jackson had time to exhaust all the reasons why federal agents stopped by his shop, the bells on the glass door clanged. Jackson looked up. It was Diego.

"Hey, Diego. How are you, my friend?" Jackson asked with a smile.

"Depends if you've got something for me," Diego shot back as he swaggered toward the glass case separating him from Jackson.

"Of course, I do. Right here." Jackson held up the betting slips. "Do you have something for me?"

Diego flipped a backpack off his shoulder and onto the counter. Packets of $100 bills spilled out. "Fifty Gs right there as promised."

"Excellent," Jackson said. "I appreciate it, Diego."

"No problem." Diego took the slips from Jackson and was about to push the door open before he turned around. "Those weren't feds were they?"

"Actually they were."

"What did they want?"

Jackson began to get nervous. "They wanted to talk to me about Carlita. They think she's here illegally."

"Pigs. I can't stand them." Then Diego walked out.

Jackson let out a big sigh of relief. He could take the feds poking around in his business. But he didn't want Diego and his gang, the Black Knights, suspecting him as a rat.

* * *

JACKSON SHUTTERED HIS SHOP at 5:30 and made the short five-minute drive to his apartment. When he went to unlock the door, he noticed it was ajar.

"Carlita? Are you here?"

Jackson noticed the house was a wreck, not characteristic of the way Carlita kept their place. He then turned toward the near corner of the room to find Diego sitting in his recliner. Diego pointed his gun at Jackson.

"What have you done?" Jackson asked.

Diego didn't say anything. He simply motioned to the corner of the room with his gun. There lay Carlita's dead body, the carpet soaked in her blood.

Jackson's face went white. He began sobbing as he moved toward her body. "How could you do this?" Jackson asked, glaring at Diego.

"Nothing personal, Jackson. We can't have anyone talking to the feds. No loose ends."

Jackson gasped for breath as he tried to process what had just unfolded. Carlita was gone. He wailed for a minute or so, throwing himself across her body.

When he finished, he wiped his tears and turned angry as he spoke.

"I didn't say anything to them about anyone. They didn't even tell me what they wanted to talk to me about."

Diego didn't get up. "I can't take any chances, Jackson. My bosses are careful people."

Diego was done explaining. He fired three shots at Jackson. Two bullets to the chest. One to his head.

Jackson collapsed to the floor.

"Nothing personal, Jackson. Just business."

* * *

WHEN ANDERSON AND GANT approached the front door of Jackson's apartment, they knew something was wrong. The door was wide open and the house was a mess. They drew their guns and announced their presence.

As they turned the corner, Anderson saw the bodies of Jackson and Carlita in the corner. He knelt down to check for a pulse. They were both dead.

"Check the house, Gant."

"All clear, Anderson. But it looks like our little gambler was trying to send us a message."

Scrawled in blood on the wall was one word: Diego.

CHAPTER 11

NOAH NEEDED TO MAKE A CALL but paranoia set in. What if they've bugged my phone? He decided not to take any chances.

He knocked on Ricky Johnson's hotel room door.

Johnson answered the door.

"What's up, man? Come on in. You all right?"

"Yeah, I'm just trying to call Ellen and I can't get a signal. You mind if I borrow your phone?"

"Sure, man. Here."

Johnson tossed his phone to Noah; it slipped out of his hand and fell onto the bed closest to the wall.

"That's why you throw the ball instead of catch it."

Noah flashed a smile and chuckled, the first time that had happened in nearly two days. He began punching in some numbers.

"Are you sure you're OK, man? The pressure isn't getting to you, is it?"

"No, I'm fine," Noah said as he began moving toward the door. "I'll be right back."

Noah returned to his room where he pulled out the card Cal handed him earlier that day and dialed the number.

"Agent Anderson," said the voice on the other end.

"Uh, yes, Agent Anderson, this is Noah Larson. Cal told me

you might be able to help me."

"Yeah, I did tell him that. Thanks for giving me a call. I want you to understand that our top priority in this case is getting your son back safe and alive. I know this is a horrible ordeal for you to be going through at any time, much less this week."

"I don't care about anything else but getting him home safely."

"I understand. And in order to do that, we need to know more about the people who have contacted you. What can you tell us about them?"

"All I know is that the guy I've spoken with has a broken English accent. He sounds like he's from Mexico or Latin America. Beyond that, I don't know much else."

"Have they sent you proof of life?"

"Yes, to my cell phone. I still have those pictures and all the messages."

"Good. Please forward them to my number. We also want to tap your phone in case they call again."

"That's fine. Do what you've got to do to catch this animal."

"We're doing our best."

"Cal also told me that you've got a lead in the case. How is that going?"

"Well, I'm not going to lie, Noah. It's rough right now. Our lead just turned up dead and all we have is a name. But we're doing our best to uncover the identity of the man responsible for this."

Noah began to tear up. He couldn't let his macho image override his paternal emotions. His sniffles were audible to Anderson.

"Don't worry, Noah. We're going to catch these guys. You've got my word on that."

"OK, thanks."

Noah hung up the phone. He could barely see the screen for all the tears blurring his vision. He transferred the images from his phone to his laptop and then emailed them to Agent Anderson. Noah then composed himself before returning Ricky's phone.

Could he hold up this week? The burden felt heavy but he had to do it. He had to put on a happy face for Jake. The world couldn't know.

* * *

CAL SIFTED THROUGH HIS NOTES from Fink about the rest of the coverage for the week. He reviewed his assignments and wondered how he could focus long enough with the biggest story of the year—if not in the history of the NFL—looming within arm's reach.

It was 9:30 p.m. when Cal checked the time on his phone. One minute later, it buzzed.

"Cal Murphy."

"Hey, Cal. It's Kelly. I finally made it. You still want to hang out tonight?"

"As a matter of fact I do. When do you think you'll be able to get together?"

"What about in an hour?"

"Sounds good. Just call me when you get to the Four Seasons lobby and I'll come down and get you."

"Great. See you in a bit."

Cal hung up. He needed to talk with someone about what was happening. The integrity of the Super Bowl was at stake. It was the story of a lifetime but Cal couldn't touch it. Not yet anyway.

* * *

THE NEXT HOUR ELAPSED QUICKLY as Cal prepared for Wednesday's coverage. At 10:30 p.m. on the nose, his phone buzzed again.

"Kelly? You here?"

"Yep. I'm in the lobby. Come on down."

Cal grabbed his room key and phone and headed downstairs.

He and Kelly had been through a traumatic experience together not that long ago. They couldn't deny the special bond between them. Was it romance? Neither could be sure. But there was an undeniable chemistry when they put their journalism heads together. They worked well together, something they hadn't done since running from crooked cops and mafia goons across Southern Idaho a few years ago.

Cal wasn't sure why he and Kelly weren't together, but he knew it would be good to see her again.

It only took him a moment to spot her by her signature long legs and warm smile.

"Cal, it's so good to see you," she said, hugging him.

"You too, Kelly. Welcome to Houston."

"Should be a fun week, eh?"

"Loads. I just can't believe you took off this much time for the game."

"Are you kidding me? The Seahawks in the Super Bowl? Who knows when this will happen again?"

"Well, you have a point."

"So, how was Media Day? I saw you on the news."

"Oh, that. It was just a big misinterpretation of events. No big deal."

Cal knew he wasn't fooling Kelly.

"Really, Cal? A misinterpretation? Is that what you're going with?"

Cal was beginning to feel uncomfortable.

"Can I buy you a drink? I'll tell you the truth once we find a quiet corner to talk."

He motioned toward the lounge with his hand.

They sat down at a table and ordered a couple of drinks before Cal began talking.

"So, what is really going on, Cal?"

"OK, listen. You can't tell anyone about this. Got it?"

"Deal. What's up?"

"I hate to tell you this, Kelly. But the Seahawks are going to lose Sunday."

Kelly laughed. "Are you kidding me, Cal? We're going to crush the Dolphins."

"No, I didn't say I *think* the Seahawks are going to lose Sunday. I *know* they're going to lose."

"What are you talking about?"

"The game is being fixed."

"Are you serious? By whom?"

"I am serious. And I don't know yet. But what I do know is that someone has kidnapped Noah Larson's son and told him that he has to lose the game if he wants to see his son alive again."

"No way! Why haven't you reported this?"

"I can't, Kelly. Not yet anyway. I've got a friend who works with the FBI who called me wondering if I'd heard any rumors about a fix. I hadn't heard any rumors but I saw a picture of Noah's son gagged pop up on his cell phone when he went to look for coffee during our interview this morning. I told Noah that I told the FBI and that's why he was angry with me. That's what the cameras captured, but no one was close enough to hear what we were really talking about."

"This is unbelievable. Do the feds know what is going on?"

"They have a few leads, but nothing definitive. This is the craziest story I've ever stumbled upon—and I can't report on it."

"Why not?"

"Well, the kidnappers told Noah that if they find out he's been talking to authorities, they are going to kill his son. They'll know he's talked if I write about it. I can't have his son's blood on my hands, all for an article."

"Wow. I don't know what to say."

"Yeah, I don't know what to think either. Fink told me to sit tight with the information, so nobody else knows about it."

"Fink is sitting on this? That's a first, but understandable, I guess. Well, look, if you need to talk more about it, I'm here for you."

She reached across the table and grabbed his hand. It felt sympathetic more than romantic. But Cal was too much of a jumbled emotional mess at that moment to decipher what a little hand touch meant.

"Thanks, Kelly. I appreciate it."

Finally sharing his burdensome secret with Kelly felt good. If only he could help Noah get his son back.

CHAPTER 12

IT WAS WELL PAST MIDNIGHT in Las Vegas when Anderson zeroed in on his new suspect, Diego. Working in the white-collar crimes division, his investigations bogged down when they collided with violent criminals. His desperation led to a Vegas bureau-wide email requesting help on a potential gang member known as Diego. A quick response by a colleague who investigated gang-related activity yielded a solid lead. He even texted a photo of the suspect along with some other information that might be helpful for gaining leverage in questioning him.

Thirty minutes later, Anderson and Gant were banging on the door of Diego's apartment. They arrested him for murder and didn't wait to interrogate him.

"I know what you did today, Diego, and I know why you did it," Anderson started. "But what I really want to know is who you're working for?"

"Trust me, man. You don't want to know."

"Oh, I think you're wrong about that. Now, who are you working for?"

"I'd rather go to jail. You don't rat out this guy."

"Oh, don't worry. You're going to jail either way. But I guess you don't care about your wife and kids going back to Nicaragua either. Just put them on a plane with no daddy and let them rot in their crime-infested hell hole."

"Hey, man. You leave my family alone. They didn't do anything."

"You tell me who you're working for and I will. Otherwise, your kids will grow up calling some other man 'daddy.' "

"OK, OK. Just promise me you'll leave them alone."

"Start talking."

"A week ago, this guy asked me to deliver three briefcases of money to a guy named Gil Jackson. They told me to come back on Tuesday and collect something for him and to give him another briefcase with money."

"Did this guy have a name?"

"Yes. His name was Javier."

"Do you know who Javier works for?"

"Yeah. Rumor is he works for the Hernandez family."

"*The* Hernandez family? The one from Juarez?"

"Yeah. That's the one. When they ask you to do something, you don't say no or else it will be the last thing you say."

Nobody said a word the rest of the ride back to the FBI offices. Anderson wanted to know how his investigation had gone from a white crime to one being directed by one of the most dangerous cartels in the western hemisphere.

CHAPTER 13

CAL'S PHONE BEGAN BUZZING. He rolled over and squinted at the screen's blinding light. *Who's calling me at 5:30 in the morning?*

"Hello?"

"Cal, I thought you said your friend at the FBI could help?"

"Noah, is this you?"

"It sure is, Cal. And I'm not happy. The FBI's lead wound up dead, and those bastards have probably already killed my son by now."

"Whoa. Slow down, Noah. When did you talk to them?"

"Last night. I called Agent Anderson like you asked me to do and he told me the lead they had was dead."

"Well, don't give up hope just yet."

"It's Wednesday, Cal. *Wednesday!* Time is running out."

"I'll give Agent Anderson a call today and find out what else is going on. Just don't panic, OK? They're going to find your son."

"You don't know that, Cal."

"You're right. I don't *know* that. But I *believe* they're going to find him. Just don't give up hope so easily."

"OK. Call me if you hear something."

"I will."

Cal hung up and rolled back into the middle of his bed. Not

that he could go back to sleep now. His mind was already wild with ideas about who was holding Noah's son and what their real motivation was behind it all. *Could this simply be about money?* It always seemed to be. That's the number one rule in investigative journalism, right? *Follow the money.* But in reality, it wasn't always that simple. Following the money had led to the FBI finding one dead lead according to Noah. Every rule had exceptions.

* * *

CAL'S NEXT SCHEDULED PRESS conference was at 12:30 p.m., giving him plenty of time to prepare for his day. He decided to wait until the sun was up in Vegas before calling Anderson.

At 9 a.m. he dialed Anderson's number.

"Cal? What are you doing calling me so early?"

"Just anxious to hear about what's going on in the case. Noah called me this morning. He crawled all over me for telling you and was panicking that your lead was found dead. Is that true?"

"Yeah, that's true. But we got another one after I spoke with him. And now we know who's behind it all."

"Really? Can you tell me who?"

"Yeah. But it won't mean anything to you. It's a name I doubt you've ever heard."

"So, who is it?"

"The Hernandez cartel. Ever heard of 'em?"

"Nope. Where are they located?"

"Juarez."

"Mexico?"

"Yeah. Crazy, huh?"

"Oh, man. That's not good."

"No, it isn't. But we're going to work on a plan this morning to rescue Jake. We've just got to find out exactly where he is first."

"OK. Good luck with that."

"I'll be in touch, Cal."

Cal hung up. In an instant his confidence in the FBI vanished.

Going into Juarez was a suicide mission. Mexican authorities notoriously refused to cooperate with U.S. law enforcement. And if they did, there were at least a dozen dirty cops on the take that would warn Hernandez. Everyone knew the cartels had the police in their pocket.

He decided to wait before he called Noah. No use in making the poor guy panic needlessly. Cal needed more facts, more substance. If he didn't have enough to write a story, he didn't have enough to tell Noah. At least for the time being.

Suddenly, covering the Super Bowl seemed like a second-rate assignment to Cal. He wanted to see these monsters brought to justice. He didn't want his enduring image of Jake to be one of him gagged and guarded by his captors.

CHAPTER 14

RIVERA STOPPED BY TO SPEAK with Hernandez before starting his shift of guarding Jake. He was anxious to relieve Morales, who didn't seem to care about the boy's welfare like he did.

"You wanted to see me, boss?"

"Yes. I wanted to let you know the plan for the boy."

"OK. Are we moving him?"

"Not yet. But I want you to dump his body as soon as the game ends on Sunday. Just throw him in the river after Morales takes care of him."

"Are you sure you want to do that, boss? Why not drop him off at the border instead? Do we need to kill him?"

"Of course we need to kill him. He's seen too much already. Did you think this was about playing daycare for the week? This is about making a ton of cash in one day. You think I care what happens to that boy? That's why I let Morales watch him. So what if he kills the kid?"

"Boss, they're going to want proof of life."

"Of course they are. And you're going to give it to him. Just don't let Morales kill him until after the game is over. Got it?"

"Got it, boss."

Rivera exited the room without another word. The walk across the compound to Jake's quarters gave him plenty of time to think. He couldn't believe Hernandez had become so ruthless. *It was a six-year-old boy!* He was innocent, a pawn caught up in an evil man's game of greed. He didn't deserve to die. But Hernandez had all but sealed Jake's fate with a chilling edict.

Just throw his body in the river ...

The words haunted Rivera as he knocked on the door to relieve Morales.

"Come on in. He's all yours," Morales mumbled.

Rivera noticed blood trickling out of the corner of Jake's mouth and a shiner on his left eye.

"What did you do?" Rivera asked in a hushed voice as he stood in the doorway.

"What? Oh, that? We were just wrestling a little bit."

"It looks like you beat him, Morales."

"So what if I did?"

"We need to keep him alive—and we need his dad to think we are treating him well instead of using him as a punching bag."

"That's why I took this picture before I beat him up." Morales held up a picture of a gagged Jake devoid of any visible physical injuries. I'll send it to you now."

Rivera fumed as Morales strode away.

"Are you OK, Jake?" Rivera asked as he shut the door.

Jake nodded. Then he started crying. Rivera pulled the gag out of his mouth.

"No, no. Don't cry. It's OK. I'm going to take care of you."

Jake pointed toward where Morales just stood. "Then make that man stop hitting me."

"Don't worry. Everything is going to be all right. You'll see your daddy soon enough." Rivera lied.

He then transferred the latest picture of Jake onto a fresh burner cell phone and sent it to Noah with another ominous message.

CHAPTER 15

ANDERSON ENTERED HIS BRIEFING on the suspicious gambling case with knots in his stomach. What was once a strange betting pattern had now devolved into a kidnapping and murder case involving one of Juarez's most dangerous cartels. He felt unqualified to lead the new interdepartmental task force to solve the case. He felt worse about the single idea he had to propose to bring Jake home alive and maintain the integrity of the Super Bowl.

He passed out a prepared briefing for everyone on the team to read, so they could familiarize themselves with the case. It contained all the facts of the case, including pictures from the grizzly murder scene the evening before. Only the rustling of papers interrupted the silence in the room before one of the agents spoke.

"So how are we going to crack the Hernandez family without the help of the Mexican government?" one of the agents asked.

"Good question," Anderson said. "I've got an angle that I think just might work."

* * *

CAL HAD JUST FINISHED covering Seattle's early afternoon

press conference when his phone rang. He found a quiet nook in the tunnel of Reliant Stadium to talk.

"Got any good news, Anderson?"

"Kind of."

"What do you mean, kind of?"

"Well, I have an idea of how we can rescue Jake."

"Excellent. I know Noah will be happy to hear that. Do you think it will work?"

"Yes, but it's contingent upon one thing."

"What's that?"

"Your help, Cal. I need you to help me."

"Anything. Just tell me what to do."

"You might not want to volunteer so quickly until you hear what it involves."

"Look, I don't care. Just tell me what it is."

"I need you to go interview Hernandez in Juarez."

"What? Are you kidding me?"

"Nope. I've already cleared it with Fink if you're willing to do it."

"What could I possibly interview him about?"

"He's got a legit coffee company that is preparing to launch in the U.S. next month. And guess what city he's starting in?"

"Seattle?"

"Yep. And all I want you to do is go interview him at his place. All you have to do is gather some information for us about his compound and we'll take care of it from there."

"OK, you do realize there's this thing called the Super Bowl I'm covering this week, right?"

"Yeah. That's why Fink is sending someone in your place."

"But the deal is, you'll be able to write this story before anyone else."

"Well, that's all I need to hear. The Super Bowl will be a Page 2 story compared to this. I'm in."

"OK, I'll email you some information. But we need you to act on this right away for this to work. Got it?"

"Yeah, got it."

"Oh and one more thing. You'll probably need to take a photographer. You think anyone at the paper would be up for this assignment?"

"Hmmm. I doubt the photographers down here would give up covering the Super Bowl for this story, but I might know someone who would do it. I'll call you after I get the information."

"Great. It's on its way now."

Cal hung up the phone. His first thoughts were about having access to writing the story of the year, if not the century. His next thoughts spiraled into what an idiot he was. Who did he think he was? This was the Hernandez family. They put people's heads on a pointy stick just for challenging them on Twitter. They hang dead bodies from overpasses. Did he have a death wish?

It took Cal a few minutes to sort everything out in his head. He finally concluded that if it were his son in this situation, he would hope someone else would have the courage to do what he was being asked to do. He didn't care to be a hero. But he did give Noah his word that he would help, and little Jake's life was at stake.

If he made it out alive, he would have one heck of a story to write.

Now he just had to convince Kelly to join him.

CHAPTER 16

CAL CALLED FINK TO LET HIM KNOW he was going to assist the FBI. Getting the opportunity to cover the Super Bowl was a cherry on top of Cal's sports writing dreams. But that was when he was young and had yet to experience the rush of covering a national story with a sinister storyline. And this was even better—it was an *international* story! There was no scenario he could have imagined where he would forfeit his Super Bowl credentials. Then again, this scenario was unimaginable.

Moments after hanging up with Fink, Cal received a text message from Josh. It read: "Thx, bro. I owe you big time." Cal knew his friend was a worthy replacement. After all, it was just another football game.

Cal sent a text message to Noah's phone, letting him know that he was helping the FBI's investigation and that he would call him with more information when he could.

With almost all the details handled, a key one remained: Kelly. How would he convince Kelly to leave behind her Seahawks in the Super Bowl and enter a dangerous faux photo shoot in Juarez at the home of a cartel boss? This might be his biggest task.

He dialed her number.

"Cal? What are you doing?" Kelly said.

"Just finished today's press conference. What are you up to?"

"Oh, just picking out an outfit for a party I'm going to tonight."

"Really? Who's throwing a party?"

"I'm not sure, but I met this guy in the lobby who gave me two tickets to a party at this swanky club downtown. Wanna come?"

"Maybe."

"Maybe? Are you kidding me? You need to have some fun this week, Cal. Enjoy the moment. This is the week of the Super Bowl. Don't be a stick in the mud."

"Well, OK. But I need to ask a big favor of you."

"What's that?"

"I kind of need your help."

"With what?"

"The FBI is asking me to play a role in getting Noah's son back."

Cal paused. Kelly remained silent. She knew there was more—and she didn't like the anticipation hanging in the air.

"And what, Cal? You want me to do something, don't you?"

"Yes. I want you to come to Juarez with me on a photo shoot."

"What? Are you crazy? The Seahawks are playing in the Super Bowl this week. The SUPER BOWL! This is like Hailey's Comet rare. I'm not going to miss it."

Cal had a hunch she would protest with something like that. He came prepared.

"OK, I understand. But why would you want to see the Seahawks play out a pre-determined script? You know they're going to lose, right? Unless I help Noah Larson get his son back, he's going to throw the game."

"Oh, no, Cal. It's not just that. This is dangerous stuff, stuff that's way over my head. I may have stumbled into it last time with you, but you're not dragging me into this."

"Where's your sense of adventure? Don't you want to reunite Noah Larson with his son? Watching the Seahawks lose in the Super Bowl won't compare to that moment—that much I can promise."

"Cal, this is not some Indiana Jones adventure. This is serious. Have you been reading about what is going on in Juarez? That place is a death trap."

"I know the risks. But getting killed is far from a foregone conclusion. Jake dying is *if* we don't do something about it."

"We? So, now this is contingent upon us? Where did this 'we' come from?"

"OK, I'm sure I can find another photographer. I don't *need* you. But I *want* you. I want you to be with me. We've done this before, this exposing the bad guys thing."

Cal's more direct appeal to her seemed to work. Kelly softened.

"Suppose I agreed to go. What would I have to do?"

"All the FBI is asking us to do is pose as reporters—which shouldn't be that hard—and gather some information on Hernandez's compound. We can do this."

"Oh, Cal. Why are you doing this to me?!"

"It's either watch the Seahawks lose, which you and I both know how miserable that makes you, or join me for an adventure in Mexico and save a little boy from certain death. Is it really that hard to choose?"

"Yes, Cal. Yes, it is. I want to relax and have fun at parties this week, not risk my life by photographing a cartel boss."

"Well, think about it and call me back. I need to know something very quickly."

Kelly paused.

"OK, I'll do it."

"You will? You sure you don't want to think about it?"

"Just take my yes, Cal, and don't make me mull it over. I might change my mind."

"Thank you, thank you! Kelly, I owe you big time."

"You sure do."

"I'll call you later this afternoon with all the details."

Cal hung up the phone and let out a big sigh. His chances were better with Kelly than anyone else.

CHAPTER 17

CAL PORED OVER THE INFORMATION Anderson sent him. Logistical details. Background notes. Contacts at the FBI's field office in Houston. Cal's final remaining hurdle was to convince Hernandez to let him conduct an interview in his home on Friday afternoon. Simple enough.

He dialed Hernandez's number.

"Hernandez."

"Hi, Mr. Hernandez. My name is Cal Murphy and I'm a reporter with *The Seattle Times*."

"Hello, Mr. Murphy. How did you get this number?"

"A good reporter never reveals his sources."

Hernandez chuckled dismissively. "Well, what can I do for you?"

"Well, we heard a rumor that your coffee, *Buenisimo!*, is coming to Seattle next month and we would love to do a story on you and your coffee for the paper."

"That sounds great. When would you like to do it?"

"What about Friday afternoon?"

"*This* Friday?"

"Yes. Does that work for you?"

"I'm sure we can make that work. You can call me back on this number then if you like."

"Oh, no. This is Seattle. We don't do phone interviews on something as serious as coffee. I would like to come to your place and talk there. I'll have my photographer with me."

"I'm not sure I can accommodate that request, Mr. Murphy. I'm very busy Friday."

"I understand. I'm in Texas covering the Super Bowl this week and my editors just heard about your coffee. They thought they could save a little on the expense account. Budgets are tight these days. So, if you can't do it, you can't do it. We won't be able to do the story any other time either."

"Well, maybe I can make it work. But I can't do a long interview. I have much business to attend to."

"I understand, Mr. Hernandez."

"OK, let's do it in the afternoon. I'll give you an hour."

"Outstanding."

"Call my assistant and she will give you all the details about what time and how to get to my place."

Cal took down all the information for Hernandez's assistant and hung up. The plan was coming together.

* * *

HERNANDEZ HUNG UP THE PHONE and summoned one of his men. He needed someone to relieve Diaz, another one of Hernandez's specialists, from watching the boy. He had a new job for his ruthless clean-up man.

Diaz's appearance frightened even the boldest bare-knuckled brawler. His baldhead had a large skull and cross bones tatted over it. A rigorous workout regiment led to bulging biceps that served as a canvas for his intimidation. He was a walking billboard for Juarez's finest tattoo parlor and every splotch of ink displayed something related to death, guns, or vague drug references. There was even one about torture. At 6-foot, 4-inches, his mean frame cast a terrifying shadow on all those in his path.

He lumbered across the compound for Hernandez's private office.

"What is it, boss?" Diaz asked as he strode into the room.

"I need you to go on a little trip for me."

"Where to?"

"Houston. I need you to look into a reporter for me. A Cal Murphy. He called me up and requested an interview suddenly. I think he might have other intentions. Tail him and find out what you can for me. You can take my plane. I'll have it gassed and ready to go by the time you get to the airport."

"You got it, boss."

Hernandez valued his prized soldier. There wasn't a thing Diaz wouldn't do for him. Diaz didn't care about getting his hands dirty—and it forever endeared him to his boss. He once cut a girl's tongue out with a butter knife because she spit at Hernandez. Another time he used a paper cutter to slice off a man's nose when he wouldn't talk. Ruthless. And loyal. There were no two better traits to get you promoted within Hernandez's organization than those two.

If Cal was lying, Diaz would find out.

CHAPTER 18

CAL AGREED TO ATTEND the mysterious Super Bowl party that evening as Kelly's date even though he was quite sure the man inviting Kelly intended for her to bring another girl. He put on his lucky suit and hoped for an evening of fun to divert his mind from the burden weighing upon him. Cal hated keeping secrets, especially the kind that belonged in the newspaper. This story stuck to him, consumed him. He couldn't stop thinking of all the possible angles, and how depraved the human race had become. There were infinite ways to make money in the world but the quickest ones always seemed like the sickest ones. Ransom a child. Sell some drugs. Cheat a client. Making money by any means necessary had overrun most every virtue. What verse did he remember the priest quoting the last time he attended mass? The *love* of money was the root of all evil? It was four years ago, but he remembered. Surely Hernandez had plenty of money, more than he could spend in a lifetime. But he loved it so much he wanted more of it. And now he had taken another man's child to ransom him for profit. Hernandez needed to pay for this.

Upon reaching the lobby, Cal immediately lost his train of thought once he noticed Kelly. *Those legs.* He knew he would have trouble preventing other men from hitting on her tonight. She looked stunning in a silky black dress accented with an elegant pearl necklace.

"Ready?" Kelly asked, smiling.

"Sure thing. You look nice. Where are we off to again?"

"Thanks, and here's the invitation card," Kelly said, handing it to him.

Cal looked outside and decided to have the concierge call a cab. The rain splashed against the lobby windows. It appeared to move in sheets horizontally across the street.

"This should be fun," Cal said.

"Are you being sarcastic, Cal? You know how I hate sarcasm."

"Guilty as charged. Can't see how you think going to some strange party in this nasty weather is going to complete your Super Bowl experience, but whatever."

"You don't have to go, you know."

"I know. It'll be all right. I just despise these functions."

"You don't even know whose party it is."

"Exactly."

"What if it's a party being thrown by Dennis Rodman?"

"Dennis Rodman? Uh, no thanks. Not interested in attending a freak show."

"What about Shaq?"

"Why do you think only NBA players can throw parties at the Super Bowl?"

"Because that's how they roll. Glitzy parties. Famous people. Expensive champagne."

"Since when do you like that stuff?"

"I don't. I just thought it'd be fun to try it once."

"Well, watch yourself tonight. This could be some party thrown by a drug dealer who slips something into women's drinks and takes advantage of them."

"You need to chill on the conspiracy theories, Cal. Just because you're right one time, doesn't mean it's always a conspiracy."

"Fine. I've just got a lot on my mind."

"I know. Just try to have some fun tonight, will you?"

The concierge motioned to Cal.

"Looks like our ride is here."

They followed the concierge out the lobby door where he shielded them from the driving rain with an umbrella. Cal tipped him as he and Kelly slid into the cab.

* * *

DIAZ EASED HIS BLACK SEDAN out of the parking space located some 20 yards from the hotel entrance. He had been waiting patiently for Cal to emerge from the building. It was just a bonus that Kelly was with him, too. He noted they looked dressed for a party, but after running surveillance missions for Mr. Hernandez for the past 12 years, he knew looks could be a faulty indicator.

He began following the cab.

CHAPTER 19

THE PARTY WAS A DUD. Cal employed his journalistic skills to learn that it was hosted by Jere Adams, a hacker-turned-computer corporation employee. A stark white room was lit with pale blue lamps. Techno music thumped the walls. Mildly attractive waitresses dressed in suggestive t-shirts with slogans like "Search my engine" on the front and the company's logo on the back. Cal amused himself by wondering where the "escape" button was. This was an unmitigated disaster.

"I would have rather gone to a Dennis Rodman party than this flop," Cal said to Kelly.

"What? I can't hear you?" Kelly responded loudly.

"Kelly, there's like 40 people here. It's not *that* loud."

Kelly smiled. Cal knew he was right but he also knew that she wasn't going to let him spoil her fun, even if the party was a bomb. Then again maybe she wanted to stay since she was easily the most gorgeous woman in the building. The nerds began descending upon her like zombies looking for their next meal. Cal had to get something to drink.

He motioned for the bartender and ordered a scotch on the rocks.

Cal looked at the man next to him, staring intently at his drink. He fit the profile for a computer genius. Mid to late 40s. Still had all his hair. Looked smart. Zero social skills.

"Do you work for Mr. Adams?" Cal inquired.

"Yes."

Oh, great. A talker. This is like talking to teenage student athletes.

"What do you do for him?"

"I'm in R&D."

"Oh, a researcher. That must be fun."

"Not really."

"Oh? Why not?"

"Well, we never get to test the things we create."

"That seems odd."

"Well, that's another division. They bring them back to me with field test results and I just have to fix them."

"So, what are you working on now?"

"I can't really talk about it. Sorry. Company policy."

"Of course, I understand."

"But I do have this one device I created on the side that I can tell you about."

"Oh, really? What is it?"

"Well, do you have kids, Mr. ...?"

"Murphy. Cal Murphy."

"Nice to meet you, Mr. Murphy. I'm James Wishert. So, do you have kids?"

"No."

"Married?"

"Hopefully one day."

"Well, one day when you get married and have kids, you will learn just how devious kids these days are. Kids used to listen to their parents, but not any more. So, we have to keep an eye on them more closely than ever before."

"You mean like spying on them?"

"Not exactly. But kind of."

"Well, what do you mean then?"

"I have three teenage daughters and I've already caught two of them with boys in their rooms."

"How did that happen?"

"Long story, but in short, you can't expect a perimeter warning system to work that well when you've got the spawns of computer geniuses trying to hook up with your teenage daughters."

"I see." Cal began to wonder just how protective this guy was of his daughters. Apparently, protective enough to install some sort of security system around the house.

"Anyway, since I'm banned from going into their rooms, I created a device that works with an app I wrote. It can look through walls up to 50 yards away and determine how many people are in the room."

"Why would you need that?"

"Don't ask. I've only had the chance to test it from 10 yards away."

"Why are you telling me this? I don't know. Didn't I overhear you tell someone you were a reporter with *The Times*?"

"Yes, I am."

"Well, maybe you can write a story about it and help me get out of working for this slave driver, Mr. Adams. You do know we were all required to be here, right? As in, I had no choice. Some guy is probably in my daughter's bedroom right now."

James amused Cal. For the simple reason that this vigilant father wrote apps to spy on his daughter. Sure, it was a little over the top, but it was a nice diversion from the gigahertz and megabite talk floating around the room.

"Well, good luck with that app, James."

"Would you mind trying it out for me? Maybe write an article about it?" James pleaded.

"I don't know, James. I'm a sports writer. I don't really cover tech stuff."

"OK, fine. Give it to your tech writer. Maybe he'll want to try it out."

"All right, I'll give it to him when I get back next week."

"Super. Here's all you need to make this work."

James placed in Cal's hand a small, black square headphone

plug that would insert into an iPhone. He also gave Cal a card with instructions on how to download the app.

"Thank you so much, Mr. Murphy. You have no idea how much this would mean to me."

"You're welcome, James."

Cal ordered another drink and scanned the room for Kelly. He couldn't see her, but he guessed she was somewhere in the middle of about twelve young men. They surrounded someone and it was either a tech superstar or Kelly. One of the men shifted to the side and Cal could see: it was Kelly.

Cal walked confidently across the room and broke up the conversation.

"You ready?" Cal asked.

"Yes, let's get out of here," she said.

Moans and groans served as the verbal protest from Kelly's impromptu fan club. But as much as she liked getting attention, Cal knew this was not her scene.

"See you later, boys," Kelly said, blowing them all a kiss.

The rain was still coming down but there was a taxi waiting outside the building. Cal ran to the cab and found it available. He motioned for Kelly to join him.

Cal gave the driver the address and then turned his attention to Kelly.

"What was *that* all about?" he asked her.

"What was *what* all about?"

"Blowing kisses to those guys? You know that's just wrong."

"Oh, Cal. I was just having fun. If I didn't know any better, I'd think you were jealous."

Cal said nothing. He looked straight ahead, watching the rhythmic wipers working hard to clear the windshield.

"You *are* jealous!" Kelly exclaimed. "I knew it. You didn't like me talking to those guys."

"Let's just go home. We've got a long day tomorrow."

Kelly smiled. She put her hand on Cal's knee. Cal didn't mind.

* * *

IT WAS 10:30 p.m. when Diaz's cell phone rang.

"Any news?" said the voice on the other end.

"No, boss. They went to some party. I couldn't get in, but it didn't look like anything important. Just tech wizards and booze. I only saw three women go in the whole time I was watching.

"Ha! Some party. Just keep me posted, Diaz."

"Sure, boss."

* * *

KELLY TOLD CAL GOODNIGHT before kissing him on the cheek. She then got out of the cab and disappeared into the hotel. That was a first. *She* had never kissed *him* before. Cal's emotions swirled. Maybe he had a chance with Kelly after all. Or maybe she was just being friendly. If she would blow a kiss to a bunch of personal space-invading nerds, how big of a deal was it that she gave him a peck on the cheek? It was probably nothing.

Cal checked his watch. He figured he could be back in his room by 11 p.m. and have a few minutes to re-read the files Anderson had sent him ahead of an early briefing at the FBI's Houston field office in the morning.

Upon returning to his room, Cal began emptying his pockets and pulled out Mr. Wishert's next big invention. He snickered. Then his curiosity got the best of him. He pulled out his iPhone and began typing in the address to download the app. Once he installed the app—one James called "X-Ray Vision"—Cal snapped the device into the headphone jack. After a couple of seconds, Cal's iPhone became an infrared device. He decided to try it out by walking down the hall and seeing what was really happening on his floor.

A quick trip to the ice machine and back let Cal know there were only six rooms with people in them. Two of the rooms appeared to have a single person asleep in them. The other four contained couples engaging in evening exercise.

This thing ought to be illegal. He removed the device from his phone and put it back in his pocket. Cal glanced at the time on his phone and realized he had lost 30 minutes playing with the device—but it was worth it. He got ready for bed and glanced through the files again before going to sleep.

CHAPTER 20

CAL MET KELLY THE NEXT MORNING in the lobby of the Four Seasons, and they waited there for an agent to pick them up. At 8:30 a.m., they were greeted by an FBI agent who led them to a black SUV. They piled into the vehicle and took off for the FBI offices.

"I need some coffee," Cal said, yawning.

"You're not the only one," Kelly added.

"There's plenty at the office. Don't you worry," the agent assured them.

The FBI offices were twenty minutes away, but it felt like it took longer as they waded through the traffic clogging up the Thursday morning commute. The extra congestion appeared to be the result of a rain-soaked highway and a hydroplaning mini-van that had plowed into the back of a semi-truck.

Cal studied the scene carefully as they rolled past it. He couldn't help but notice the driver's nervous eyes reflected in the rearview mirror.

"Is everything OK?" Cal asked the driver.

"Yeah. Why?"

"It looks like you keep checking to see if someone is following us. Nobody is following us are they?"

"I don't think so. I'm always extra cautious though."

Cal slumped back in his seat. He nervously bounced his knee. Kelly put her hand on his leg. He calmed down.

"Everything is going to be fine, Cal. Nobody is following us."

* * *

DIAZ STRUGGLED TO KEEP UP with the black SUV weaving in and out of traffic. It was such an unorthodox path that he wondered if he had been spotted. It was either that or Cal and Kelly were being driven by a professional. After 15 minutes he gave up. His mission in Houston was complete.

He dialed Hernandez's number.

"Boss, it's me."

"What is it, Diaz?"

"This morning, a black SUV with government plates picked up Cal and his lady friend from his hotel. I was tailing the driver but he lost me."

"Very well then. Come back at once. I need you here. I'll ready the plane for you."

Diaz hung up but he didn't head for the airfield. He wanted to give his boss a special surprise.

* * *

AFTER FIVE MINUTES, Cal was finally convinced that his paranoia was getting the best of him. Nobody was following him. He was Cal Murphy, the little sports writer from Seattle. His life was insignificant. Killing him would serve no purpose. Neither would taking him hostage. All he had to do was pretend to be writing a story on Hernandez's legitimate business, treat it like a real story, and gather some information for the feds so they could rescue Jake. It was simple. No one would get hurt. No one would know what he was doing.

BAM!

Cal lurched forward as did Kelly when the car slammed into them from the back. Tires screeched. Glass shattered. People screamed. In less than three seconds, Cal had gone from a courageous crime fighter to a discombobulated passenger. Kelly wasn't moving. Neither was the driver.

Cal scrambled to unbuckle himself and began looking for a gun. *This couldn't be a random accident. This was malicious.* Cal grabbed the unconscious agent's gun and crouched down in the back seat. He peeked over the seat and out the back window to see if anyone was coming. There was no one around.

Clang!

Cal jumped as he heard metal clinking against the pavement. Cal wondered if someone was outside the vehicle preparing for an ambush. He cocked the handgun.

He decided to poke his head out the window and see if he could see anything on the ground.

The next think Cal knew, he was being ripped from the vehicle and thrown across the pavement. The gun skidded across the pavement and under another car nearby. Cal looked up to see a hooded man looming over him. The man appeared to have no weapon, but Cal didn't want to stick around to find out if he was right. There was only one reaction: run!

Just as the man bent down to pick him up, Cal rolled out of arm's length before leaping up and hitting a dead sprint four strides into the run. He reached for his pocket and pulled out his cell phone. He dialed 911 and put the call on speaker. In between rings, Cal could hear his attacker breathing hard several yards behind him. Once the dispatcher answered, Cal decided to yell out the pertinent information instead of waiting for her questions.

"I'm being chased by a large Hispanic man going west on 43rd near the intersection of Antoine! I need someone to help me now! He's trying to kill me!"

By this point, Cal had changed directions and was now running along the sidewalk headed north on Antoine Drive. Being stuck in a residential zone could put others at risk if it became a hostage situation and Cal knew this wasn't good for anybody. But at the moment, it simply felt like a hunting expedition—and he was the prey. He had to find a very public place. The more Texans he ran into, the more chance he had of finding someone with a gun who would stop the beast hunting him.

Cal spotted a Whataburger restaurant and darted inside. He sat down and looked out the window to see if the man had followed him. He hadn't. The man was gone. Cal gasped for breath as two young boys stared at him.

"Are you OK, mister?" one of the boys asked.

"I am now," Cal said. Who knew how long it would be safe there or if Kelly and the FBI agent were safe. But for now, the busy fast-food restaurant served as a safe haven.

Cal sat in a booth and tried to catch his breath. What had just happened? Who was that man and why was he trying to kill him? It had to be one of Hernandez's men. Who else could want him dead? Or was it a case of mistaken identity?

Before Cal could mull any possibility for very long, he heard a faint voice.

"Hello? Is anyone there? Hello?"

My cell phone!

Cal fished his phone out of his pocket and began talking to the 911 dispatcher.

"Hi, ma'am. My name is Cal Murphy. I'm OK, but I don't know about my friends. I was riding in an FBI vehicle before we were rammed by someone and then attacked."

"Where are you?"

"I'm at the Whataburger off Antoine Drive."

"OK, sit tight. Officers are on their way."

* * *

THE NEXT TWO HOURS CRAWLED by for Cal. As he sat in the parking lot of the Whataburger restaurant, local police and FBI asked him question after question about the events that unfolded. As a reporter, he was used to absorbing as many details as possible about the scene. It was important to setting up the story. But he was also used to writing about it once and being done with it, not retelling suit after suit what had happened.

All he really cared about was Kelly. Nobody knew what had happened to her. Was she OK? Was she dead? Was she missing?

Cal didn't stop worrying about her until Kelly walked up to him.

"You're OK?" he said, hugging her tightly.

"I'm fine. And you?"

"That animal chased me down the street and I didn't lose him until I slipped into the restaurant."

"There's a good headline in this story somewhere."

Cal wasn't ready to laugh about it yet, but he managed a smile out of courtesy to Kelly.

"What happened to you?"

"I hit my head pretty hard. It stunned me for a few seconds, but I'm OK. I wanted to help you but when I got up and saw that guy attacking you, I figured my best chance at survival was pretending to be dead or unconscious."

"Thanks a lot."

"What? You seriously think I could've helped you?"

"Not really, but it sounds bad when you say it out loud like that."

"Well, it looks like our driver is the only one that sustained any kind of serious injuries. He's at the hospital now. They said he suffered a concussion, but he'll be fine."

"That's good news. So, do you know what's next?"

"I have no idea. I'm sure this isn't how they planned it."

"Let's hope not."

It was only 11 a.m., but the day felt complete already to Cal. Could he still go to Juarez? Would the FBI still want him to go?

Another agent made eye contact with Cal and began walking straight toward him.

"Cal?" the agent asked, offering his hand.

"That's me. And you are …?" Cal responded, shaking the man's hand.

"Agent Solterbeck. I'm running point on this investigation now since everything is shifting to our region. I'm still working with Agent Anderson in Vegas, but I'm calling the shots from here on out. I was also scheduled to brief you on the operation in Juarez a few hours ago before this untimely accident."

"You're just calling this an accident?! Some guy yanked me through a car window and tried to kill me!"

Solterbeck motioned for Cal to keep it down. "We don't want the local police force knowing about this. Let's keep this hush-hush. We think there might be a gang informant on the force."

"So, you think this was gang-related and had nothing to do with Hernandez?" Cal asked.

"We're not sure what we know at this point. But what we *think* we know is that Agent Barber was being watched by a gang he's been investigating for weeks now. We think they may have suspected you were his key witnesses."

"You think this was all a case of mistaken identity? I'm not sure I'm buying that."

Solterbeck lied. "That's what it appears to be at this point. Did you get a good look at the guy? Think you could identify him again?"

"He was wearing a mask, but he did have this funky Spanish tattoo on his arm. It said, 'La Pelona.' Never heard that word before. Does that mean anything to you?"

Solterbeck lied again. "Nope, but I'll have our team look into it. And listen, we still need you to go to Juarez if you're up for it. It's not like Jake's life depends on it or anything."

Cal just shook his head. He looked at Kelly, her mouth gaping. Cal couldn't believe that the FBI had truly pinned their hopes of saving Jake on he and Kelly's fake interview.

"We're all you've got?" Cal asked. He couldn't hide the incredulity in his voice.

"You are for now, Cal. Let's go. I've got a car waiting for you two over there."

Cal and Kelly started walking toward a car in the direction Solterbeck had pointed.

"Can you do this after what you just went through, Kelly?" Cal asked.

"I'm fine. I really want to help Jake get back to his dad."

"OK. As long as you're OK with it, I guess I am, too."

They both climbed into the car and waited to be transported to the FBI offices just a few short blocks away.

* * *

"DIAZ, WHERE ARE YOU? The pilot has been waiting on you for over an hour?"

"I got stuck in traffic, boss."

"OK, well hurry it up. I need you back here right away."

Diaz ended the call. It wasn't the first time he had lied to Hernandez, nor would it be the last. But that's why he liked to surprise his boss rather than make promises he couldn't always keep. The boss bought his excuse. He'd be in Juarez in an hour. All would be forgotten. It's not like he wouldn't get another chance at the two journalists.

CHAPTER 21

ON A BREAK DURING THE FBI BRIEFING, Cal called Noah and left a message. He wanted Seattle's most popular professional athlete to know he was risking his own life to save his son. Even while he was leaving the message, Cal felt strange about it. He didn't want to brag or seem like some hero, but he did want Noah to appreciate the sacrifices he was making to save Jake.

Five minutes after he left the message, he received a text from Noah: "Thx."

Cal felt like complaining to Kelly about it but then thought it would make him sound like a whiny brat. *That's it? A simple three-letter text response?* Instead, he began pondering a better question: What were *his* true motivations? To be a hero and get an award-winning story? Or to help a dad get his son back? It shouldn't have been a question Cal had to ask—and if he was asking it, maybe the answer wasn't so noble. This couldn't be about him. It had to be about Jake and Noah and nothing else. If something else beneficial to his career came out of this, then great. But he had to get the proper mindset: He would do this if no one else ever heard about it or read about it. This wasn't about him.

Cal returned to the briefing room and sat down next to Kelly.

"You think you can do this?" Cal asked her again.

"Geez, Cal, I'm not some China doll. I think you know I can

handle myself. Why else would you have asked me to go?"

Cal smiled. He wanted to answer her rhetorical question but decided against it. There were multiple reasons why he wanted her to go. If she couldn't figure that out, she wasn't as smart as Cal gave her credit for being.

To Cal, Kelly's fiery spirit was more attractive than her striking outward appearance. Her mom once told Cal about Kelly's first co-ed soccer practice. After 30 minutes, Kelly realized the boys were not passing her the ball. She ended that with an impromptu speech about how they better start passing her the ball and just because she was a girl was no excuse to leave her out. The next pass went to her and she buried the ball in the back of the net. She finished the season as the team's second-leading scorer. That attitude made Kelly stand out in a crowd. She could be a dainty princess one minute, a Marine commander the next. She was her own woman—and she was going to make a fine partner on this operation in Juarez.

The briefing last another 30 minutes and wrapped up just before one o'clock.

"Your plane leaves in two hours," Solterbeck said, handing the journalists a packet with their itinerary and contacts in Juarez. "You'll find your new agency issued passports as well. Getting in and out of the country will be a breeze for you with these. Any final questions?"

"Nope. I think we've got a good idea of what we're supposed to do: locate where they are holding Jake and tell you what we can about the compound."

"That's it. Good luck, you two."

* * *

MR. HERNANDEZ HEARD THE TIRES bark as his Gulfstream G450 touched down on his personal runway, and he headed outside. Having a place to land your private jet meant dispensing with government employees. The amount he saved on bribes alone for officials at Gonzalez International more than paid for the paved strip.

He stood near the door and waited for Diaz to exit.

"How was your flight?" Hernandez asked as Diaz began lumbering down the plane's steps.

"Good."

"So, we have much to discuss, starting with how we're going to dispense of Mr. Murphy and his lady friend."

"It will be my pleasure." Diaz snarled and cast a menacing gaze toward his boss.

Hernandez had seen this look only once before from Diaz. It came when a member of the Menendez cartel nearly killed him. A few weeks later, Hernandez found the man in his compound, tied to a chair and barely alive. Diaz had cut off the man's fingers and used them to gouge his eyes out. Five years later, the image still haunted Hernandez.

"What really happened in Houston, Diaz?"

Diaz ignored the question. "How are we going to dispense of Mr. Murphy?"

Hernandez shuttered. He knew Diaz's thirst for revenge would only be quenched one way.

"Let's go inside and talk."

CHAPTER 22

CAL AND KELLY FLEW WEST across Texas and landed at
the Biggs Army Airfield. Flying into Biggs saved them at least an
hour of dealing with airport processing. Solterbeck wanted to give
them as much time as possible to identify a good extraction point
should things go awry.

Solterbeck remained in Houston but another FBI agent had accompanied them on the flight and drove them to the border.

"Remember, we have agents in Juarez, but we don't want you
to contact them unless it's an emergency," he said as they stopped
near the customs gate. "Until your interview tomorrow afternoon,
check in every hour with a text message per the instructions in
your briefing so we know you're safe. Otherwise, a team will respond immediately and pull you out. Got it?"

"Got it," Cal said.

"Be safe."

With that, Cal and Kelly got out of the car and walked through
the pedestrian gate and into Juarez. They disappeared into a sea
of people streaming along the sidewalk. Two blocks later, they
came to a parking lot and identified the car that had been left for
them. They threw their belongings into the car and headed for
the hotel.

"You still OK?" Cal asked.

"Well, it's a little more real now," Kelly said. "Let's just say I'm slightly more scared now than I was when we were running for our lives through Idaho corn fields."

Cal nodded. Escaping from a single thug on their turf seemed much more manageable than infiltrating a dangerous cartel and delivering life-saving information.

"But it is kind of exciting, isn't it?" Kelly said.

"I don't know if that's the word I would use for it."

"The adventure, the rush of being in the middle of danger—don't you find that exciting?"

"I guess I like my excitement a little less life-threatening."

"That's why you write and I shoot photos."

"What does *that* mean?"

"You just like to sit back and contemplate the right words to describe something. I don't need words. I just capture the moment in its raw form."

"Aww, geez. You've got to be kidding me. It takes no skill to snap a photo."

"That's where you're wrong, Cal. Framing the moment takes way more skill than it does to use a thesaurus to find a different word for 'beautiful' or 'incredible.' Besides, what's a picture? A thousand words? I can write the equivalent of a thousand words with the touch of a button."

"That's exactly my point. It takes me a couple of hours to write a thousand words."

Kelly laughed. "A thousand words that nobody reads."

The car lurched to a stop behind a flatbed truck carrying a mix of goats, chickens and bed mattresses. A young boy clinging to one of the goats scowled at them.

Cal turned and looked intently at Kelly. He wasn't sure if she was needling him for fun or serious.

"Are you really gonna go there?" he finally asked.

"Oh, Cal. You're way too serious about your craft. Lighten up."

She then pointed her camera at Cal and took his picture.

"Nice expression, Cal. I think this is a keeper." She paused.

"Now, how many words have you written today?"

Cal shook his head and smiled. Her playful banter took the edge off the situation. He was serious about his craft. So was she. But what they were about to do had less to do with the fine art of writing or photography and more to do with the precision of investigative journalism. They needed to gather hard facts and insightful information from their interview with Hernandez. And they needed to snoop around his compound without raising suspicion.

* * *

NOAH DIALED HIS WIFE'S CELL phone number. The call went to her voicemail.

"Honey, please call me," Noah said. "I need to talk to you. The FBI is going to try and rescue Jake tomorrow night. I don't know how much longer I can pretend like everything is fine. Call me. Please."

He hung up.

Just over 72 hours remained until the Super Bowl kickoff and Noah could hardly make sense of the jumbled thoughts rattling around in his head. He couldn't concentrate. His preparation for Sunday's game was so poor that he thought his performance might not have to be faked. *I just might lose to the Dolphins because I'm not ready.*

But nothing else mattered really. *The Super Bowl didn't matter.* There wasn't a moment in his life until this week where he would have ever thought such a thing. But it didn't matter. It was just a game, a bunch of grown men acting like kids and getting paid handsomely to do it. So what that a hundred million people were going to be watching it—it was only a game.

But Jake was his son, his only son. That mattered more than anything in the world to Noah. He and Ellen struggled to get pregnant and thought it would never happen. Fertilization treatments. Surgeries. None of it worked. If they wanted any children, they would have to adopt, at least that's what the doctors said. But biological children? Forget it. Out of the realm of possibility.

Then the unimaginable happened. A year to the day after their last visit to a fertility specialist, Noah and Ellen rode out to the beach together. They wanted to bury their dream together, cast it out to sea in a bottle. They needed to do something therapeutic as a couple, to put a stake in the ground and say that being without biological children wouldn't define who they were as a couple or their marriage. They had decided to adopt and it was time to let go of the past and look forward. So they bottled their dream and Noah chucked it into the chilly Pacific waters. It was gone.

On the way home, Ellen got sick. She asked Noah to pull over so she could throw up. He got out with her and held her hair back as she heaved. Then she cried and slumped into his arms. The emotional experience had been too much for her.

Later that evening, Ellen told Noah she needed to go to the grocery store to grab a few essentials. She returned with a pregnancy test kit. She took it and it registered as pregnant. Her scream from the upstairs bathroom in their home sent Noah bounding up the stairs.

"What is it, honey?" he asked.

"We're pregnant!"

Noah felt like he had thrown a touchdown to win the Super Bowl on the last play of the game. It was an exhilarating high.

But now here he was about to actually play in the Super Bowl and he had sunk to the lowest he'd ever felt in his life. Even lower than when doctors told them they would never get pregnant. His son's life was hanging in the balance—and there was nothing he could do about it but hope and pray.

CHAPTER 23

CAL WAS SETTLING INTO HIS ROOM across the hall from Kelly when his phone rang. It was Josh.

"Hey, Josh. How are you enjoying Houston?" Cal asked.

"Man, this is incredible, but I was calling to give you my condolences about your aunt."

My aunt? Cal wondered if that was some cover story Fink created.

"Yeah, it's been rough. She was a good woman."

"Well, I'm sorry to hear about her passing—and sorry for you that it had to happen on this week."

"We knew it was coming soon, just not so soon."

"That's too bad."

"Yeah, well, don't screw up the coverage, OK? This is a big break for you."

"Don't worry. I won't mess it up. The only thing is they stuck me on the Dolphins beat this week."

"You're ready to be a real sports writer—you're covering the Super Bowl and whining already."

"Yeah, well being forced to listen to Steve Spurlock ramble on about how he's the best quarterback in the game would make anyone complain."

"That's what he's saying?"

"Yeah, this guy has an ego fitting for this state. I wish someone would remind him that the Dolphins are only in the Super Bowl because the Steelers fumbled away the game, not because of something he did. From the way Spurlock talks, you would think Sunday's outcome is a foregone conclusion."

Cal was quiet. It would be a foregone conclusion unless he helped the FBI save Jake.

"Well, good luck with everything. I'll see you soon."

"Later."

Cal ended the call. He hated lying to his best friend, but he knew Josh. And Josh wouldn't keep quiet about his situation. In less than 24 hours, this whole mess would be over with.

* * *

RIVERA RELIEVED MORALES OF HIS SHIFT, but not before demanding some answers about the state of Jake's room. Jake sat in a corner, quietly sobbing.

"What happened here?" Rivera asked.

The primitive room looked like a bomb had exploded in it. Jake's bed frame had been split in the middle and was unusable. The lone table and chair brought in for Jake to use for coloring and other activities to pass the time lay splintered on the concrete floor.

"Did you do this?" Rivera asked again when Morales refused to respond.

"No."

"Who did then?"

"Diaz."

"Is he crazy? He doesn't need to do this to the kid?"

"Look, you need to ask yourself if you've got the *cajones* to do this. Hernandez is going to test you after he gets his money." Morales leaned in close to Rivera to deliver a message in a whispered voice. "He's going to make you kill Jake."

Morales then pushed Rivera aside and exited the room, slamming the door behind him.

Rivera knelt down beside Jake.

"Are you OK, little buddy?"

Jake looked up. His shiner was almost gone but there was a long scratch across his forehead. A trail of dried blood marred his face.

"Who did this to you?" Rivera asked.

Jake didn't answer the question. "You said they wouldn't hurt me any more—and they did." Jake burst into tears, sobbing and moaning. "I want my daddy!"

Rivera couldn't believe he was doing this. Guarding a little boy like he was an animal. Treating him like one, too. It was disgusting. But he knew that if he didn't do what Hernandez said, it would be his son in a similar predicament.

However, Rivera knew he could never kill the boy. He had to draw the line somewhere. He had to think of a way out.

CHAPTER 24

HERNANDEZ SWIRLED THE TEQUILA around in his glass. Mr. Murphy presented a small kink in his plan. It could have been worse, but it wasn't: Mr. Murphy was coming to his house. It gave Hernandez every possible advantage. He could control everything about the situation. The reporter and his lady friend would be helpless pawns in his game—just like the quarterback.

"Let me finish them off, boss," Diaz said.

"And how do you propose to do that?" Hernandez asked.

"I'll just take them to the shed and beat them to death."

"I was thinking about something a little more discreet, something that wouldn't draw any attention to us. We do run a legitimate business here after all."

"So what's your idea, boss?"

Hernandez paused. That's what he liked to hear. His ideas were always the best. That's why he was the boss.

* * *

CAL AND KELLY SECURED their valuables in a safe in their rooms and proceeded to the lobby together. They needed to find a place to meet up in case they were separated or if they needed to be extracted. While Cal remained fearful of what might happen in the next 24 hours, he couldn't help feeling a little bit excited about playing spy games with Kelly.

Their hotel faced a small square with a grassy tree-lined park in the center. The cobblestone pathways extending in all directions from the center of the park would have been a nightmare for rollerbladers—or anyone else trying to navigate a wheeled device. Large tufts of grass sprouted between the bricks. Gaps of missing bricks reminded Cal this wasn't some pristine park in Seattle. This was Mexico.

At the far corner of the square sat San Augustín Chapel, a plain Catholic church. Scaffolding covered up most of the front of the church as construction crews repaired the cracking façade. Cal remembered he had actually heard about this particular church in the news a few months before when a fire gutted the inside but left the *Virgen de Guadeloupe* unscathed. The story amused Cal. He thought people believed what they wanted to believe. And if they wanted to believe that God spared a statue of Mexico's patron saint—while letting the crucifix of Jesus burn to a crisp— then so be it. Some false beliefs are unhelpful but harmless.

"Let's check out that church," Cal suggested.

"OK. Good idea."

Cal and Kelly walked across the square and toward the church in silence. The idea that they were in one of Mexico's most dangerous cities instead of enjoying Super Bowl festivities still bewildered Cal. He noted the scenery with great detail—the elderly men playing chess in one corner of the park, the boys kicking a soccer ball, the mother carrying her baby on her back. It looked so peaceful.

They crossed the street to enter the church. Cal gestured for Kelly to enter first.

The interior of San Augustín Chapel did not match the outside. Although gutted by the fire it had been completely rebuilt. The trusses spanning the width of the building displayed detailed carvings of saints and other biblical scenes. Magnificent artwork adorned the walls, depicting the lives of different saints. There was even a new painting by a local artist that showed fires leaping around the Virgen de Guadeloupe statue but not touching it. Cal continued to scan the sanctuary for places to hide or meet should it be necessary. Lost in his analysis, Cal didn't see the priest approaching.

"May I help you, señor?"

Cal looked down to see a short older man wearing a robe.

"Oh, I don't think so, Father. I'm just admiring the beautiful architecture."

The priest smiled.

"Well, I don't know if I'd go as far to say that it's beautiful, but it's certainly practical." Nodding, the padre continued. "So are you new to our parish?"

"Oh, no. I'm just visiting here on business."

"Feel free to take a look around and pardon our construction. Let me know if you have any questions."

Cal started to walk away and stopped. He turned back toward the priest who hadn't moved.

"Actually, Father, I do have a question for you." A warm smile invited Cal to continue. Why do you think bad things happen to good people?"

"Oh well, my goodness. I was expecting something more like, 'Where are the restrooms?' But you start with the difficult questions first. I like that."

Cal looked up to see Kelly slowly working her way along the artwork at the far corner of the room.

"Let me ask you a question first, my son: Why do you ask such a question?"

Cal shifted his weight back and forth and rested his hand on his chin, contemplating how to answer the Father's question.

"Well, I have this friend whose son was kidnapped one time. He was six. They traumatized him. They screamed, yelled, threw things at the poor child. He made it out alive but he didn't deserve any of it. And I just wonder why God would let such a horrible thing happen to an innocent little boy."

"Perhaps God didn't let it happen."

"Yeah, but if God is all powerful and so good, why didn't he do something to stop them?"

"I see you are deeply troubled by this. This dilemma is hard for even the most devout to understand. Especially when the evil touches them. I find a lot of people think God should be like a magic genie from a fairy tale. They just want him to make everything perfect. Poof! Throw a few lightning bolts or whatever it takes to stop evil things from happening. But have you ever considered that maybe that's a mistaken perception of God, that maybe he wants us to partner with him to do good. Maybe there is value in the struggle to overcome the evil and selfishness in our own lives. Could it be that our struggle to oppose evil by choosing good is necessary to create something beautiful in us?"

Cal didn't have an answer. He had a million questions about God and he wanted to argue with the priest, but oddly the old man's wisdom made some strange sense. His answer was worth pondering.

The priest continued.

"As the Patron Saint of our chapel once said, 'God judged it better to bring good out of evil than to suffer no evil to exist.' Perhaps God has done more good than you give him credit for. Maybe he stopped greater evil from happening to your friend's son by sending someone to rescue him. We, who question, have no way of knowing the full story."

Cal froze. It was his job to always know the full story before reporting it. And it was hard to realize that he didn't know the full story now. He knew every detail, down to the men's names and addresses who were holding Jake for ransom. But he was stepping into Noah and Ellen and Jake's story. He was stepping into the story of a Super Bowl that was fixed. He was stepping into something that hadn't yet been written. Could his desire to see justice done in this situation be divinely inspired? Cal hadn't considered that possibility. Maybe the priest was right. Maybe God was using him to do good. The idea was both overwhelming and horrific at the same time. What if he failed? What if Jake died?

"Son? Son?"

Cal's rumination on this idea had left him in a trance.

"Sorry, Father. I was just thinking about what you said. Thanks for your time."

"My pleasure, my son."

Kelly had finished working her way around the inner walls of the church and was now standing next to Cal.

"You ready, Cal?"

"Yeah, let's go."

They turned toward the exit.

"What were you and the Father talking about?"

"Stories. They always seem to get worse before they get better."

With that, the pair of journalists stepped into the bright sun and crossed the street toward the park.

"I think that's our rendezvous point if anything happens. What do you think?" Cal said.

"I agree. San Augustín Chapel it is."

CHAPTER 25

CAL TWISTED AND TURNED in his bed. His mind raced with possibilities of what the next day would bring. He thought about what the priest said. If Cal had his way, he would write a satisfying ending and be done with the mystery. It was fun to uncover the unknown. It was painful to anticipate it. Especially when the unknown consisted of walking into the home of one of the most ruthless cartel bosses in the world.

Eventually, Cal stopped thinking about the dangers lurking in the shadows. He would face evil head on—and the FBI would rescue Jake. That was the story he wanted to write. And he wanted to write it so it would appear on the front page of every newspaper in America on the morning of Super Bowl Sunday. He finally drifted off to sleep.

* * *

CAL MET KELLY FOR BREAKFAST downstairs in their hotel. They exchanged pleasantries before going over plans for their 2 p.m. meeting at Hernandez's estate.

"So, you know what you're doing, Kelly?"

"Yeah, I'm taking pictures and you're pretending to interview Hernandez."

Cal sighed. "Do you have to mock my profession?"

She laughed and winked at him.

Cal finished going over the plan, which was simple: identify where they could possibly be keeping Jake. The FBI suspected a certain building, but wanted to make sure before sending in a tactical team. With Cal and Kelly on the ground, they could ask to see certain parts of the property and better ascertain the exact location based on the openness of Hernandez's response.

Cal trusted his instincts heading into the interview, but he also didn't mind an assist from technology: James Wisher's X-Ray Vision app. The device was unassuming and Cal already had a story about how it helped him record interviews. He knew he could get away with using it if he could get close enough to one of the buildings on the perimeter. Getting within 50 yards didn't seem like it would be a problem. It was better than any tool the FBI offered and less conspicuous too.

Cal checked his watch. It was 9 a.m. and time for him to check in with his FBI handler. As he got up from the table, two teenage boys collided with him. Cal tumbled to the floor. He spun around to watch the boys dash away with his iPhone.

"Hey! Stop those kids!" Cal yelled.

Nobody moved. The four other patrons in the restaurant barely looked up from their breakfast plates.

Cal scrambled to his feet and raced off after them. He caught sight of them slipping out a back door. The door opened into a side street and by the time Cal opened it, the street was empty.

He started to panic at first about the phone and then about Kelly. In his desperation to catch the two thieves, he left her all alone, vulnerable.

When Cal returned to the table, he was out of breath.

"Oh, thank God you're fine," he said as he pulled out his chair to sit down again.

"Really, Cal? You're going to do this whole macho save-the-girl routine? I can take care of myself."

"I know. I know. I'm just on edge, OK? And I need your phone now?"

"Why?"

"I've got to check in or else they're going to pull us out."

Kelly handed her phone to Cal. He pecked out a text message for their handler, alerting him of the new situation.

"It gets worse before it gets better, right?" Kelly quipped.

Cal didn't laugh.

* * *

IT WAS ALMOST NOON and Hernandez had just finished handing out orders to his men. Rivera had been instructed to watch Jake and would get his instructions from Diaz. He poked his head out of the door in time to see Diaz striding across the property toward him.

"You can go see Hernandez now," Diaz said.

"I thought you were going to tell me what to do," Rivera said.

"I just did. Go see Hernandez."

Diaz slammed the door behind him. He growled at Jake. Rivera could hear Diaz's threats through the wall.

"If you want to see your mommy and daddy again, you better keep quiet this afternoon. You got it?" boomed Diaz.

Rivera pictured little Jake nodding his head and wiping away his tears. He couldn't imagine his own son being treated that way. It's why he had to detach himself emotionally every time he guarded the kid.

Rivera walked toward the house to see Hernandez. He didn't know how much more he could stomach watching Jake. Any new orders would be a welcome relief.

He knocked on the door to Hernandez's office.

"Come in," Hernandez said.

"You wanted to see me, boss?" Rivera questioned.

"Yes, Rivera. Have a seat. I have a new assignment for you."

"Is it about the kid?"

"Yes. He's been through enough and we don't need Diaz or Morales torturing him any more. I know you'll make it quick and painless for him, right?"

"Yes sir, boss."

Rivera started to feel sick. He couldn't kill Jake and he knew it.

"Oh, and there's one more thing I need you to do."

Rivera sat back down.

CHAPTER 26

CAL AND KELLY DROVE to Hernandez's property using a route selected by the FBI. The lack of side roads would make it difficult for Hernandez to capture the journalists and transport them to another place. There were a handful of FBI agents scattered along the road, watching for any suspicious activity. As soon as they established where Jake was, those same agents would move in and break him out of the compound.

The road remained mostly unused, as there were more direct paths. It wound along a small river that supplied irrigation to rows and rows of crops dotting the countryside. Primitive farms interrupted the wealthy farmers' landscape. It was easy to spot the difference as the scenery changed from precise rows of singular crops to no discernable rows at all. Subsistence farming versus commercial farming.

"Who lives out here?" Cal finally wondered aloud.

"Looks like lots of poor farmers who live off the land—and lots of wealthy farmers who own everything else," Kelly answered.

"Whoever they are, it's a great place to hide from the government."

Cal veered onto the prescribed dirt path as their car bumped along the dusty road. The only identifying mark was a small sign: Hernandez.

They could see the compound ahead. It appeared to be at least three-quarters of a mile away, a sprawling hacienda constructed in traditional Spanish style. Red barrel roof tiles. Stucco façade. Winding staircases on the exterior of the house leading to a balcony with a view. A bubbling ornate fountain. Cobblestone circular driveway. If a Hollywood producer wanted to film a scene at the home of a Mexican drug dealer, they couldn't have imagined a more perfect setting.

One of the gardeners paused from trimming the three-foot hedge that enclosed the long driveway. Cal's paranoia began to escalate. He wondered if they were walking into a trap, as if the gardener might drop his clippers and pull out an automatic weapon. Cal started losing his confidence quickly.

"I don't know about this, Kelly. I've got a bad feeling."

"Oh, Cal. Would you just chill out? Act normal. Interview this piece of garbage and let's get out of here so the professionals can do the dirty work."

Cal just shook his head. The trip down the driveway felt to him more like an inmate marching down death row to the electric chair. He knew they needed to act fast. He asked Kelly to text a message to their handler letting him know they had arrived and they would be dark for the next 90 minutes. She then erased the sent folder and slipped the phone into her camera bag. Extreme caution was required.

When they got out of the car, an attractive lady wearing a *Buenisimo!* nametag greeted them.

"Hi, my name is Iselda," she said offering her hand first to Cal and then Kelly. "I'll be showing you around the property today before your meeting with Mr. Hernandez."

"I thought we had a one o'clock interview?" Cal asked, growing more uneasy with each passing second.

"Oh, you do. But he won't be able to join us for another fifteen minutes. He had a conference call that is running a little late."

Cal relaxed momentarily. It sounded plausible enough. He looked at Kelly. She didn't seem bothered at all by anything. Cal took a deep breath and began following Iselda.

"So, you're from *The Seattle Times?*" Iselda asked.

"Yes," Cal said.

"I hear they make great coffee there," she said.

"The best in the world."

"Well, not quite the best." She turned and winked coyly at Cal.

Cal wondered if this is how Hernandez did it. Send out the pretty lady. Charm them. And then slit their throats. Or maybe she was going to do it. He certainly didn't suspect her. Maybe she did all his dirty work. Cal's guard went back up.

While the house was the crown jewel of the property, there were several smaller homes located nearby.

"Who lives in these houses?" Cal asked.

"Most of our staff remains on the property at all times. Cooks, gardeners, wait staff, drivers. Even Mr. Hernandez's pilots live here full-time."

Cal couldn't find any part of this story that didn't make sense or at least appeared to be true. And judging from the sprawling complex, it would take a small city to run things.

As Cal glanced around, he saw a small stable. Growing up in Idaho, Cal lived down the road from several horse breeding farms. He knew a horse stable when he saw one.

"Does Mr. Hernandez have any horses?" Cal asked.

"Actually, no. He doesn't have time for horses. The previous owner of this property had horses, which is why you see that barn. But there are no horses currently being housed there."

They rounded the corner of the house where Iselda was ready to show off the floral grounds. But Cal glanced back at the barn. He saw a large man open a side door and let another man in. Two seconds later, another man exited.

Was that a shift change? That must be where they are keeping Jake! Cal observed that the barn had curtains in the windows and looked very functional even though there wasn't a horse to be found.

Kelly walked in front of Cal. She was snapping pictures left and right of the back patio and adorning trellises. The view was magazine worthy. A wooden fence marked the rear of the property and looked as if it flowed into rolling hills. But that wasn't the case. There was a drop of about 150 feet into a ravine below, adding to the mystique of the property. The wooden post fence made it seem so serene and open. But the truth was Mr. Hernandez didn't want any one on his property without him knowing.

When Iselda turned her back, Cal tapped Kelly on the shoulder.

"Shoot a picture of the barn behind me. I know that's where they are keeping him," he whispered. It was barely audible but Kelly understood.

She knelt down to take a close-up of a flower but Cal knew she was focusing her lens elsewhere. Just as she was taking the picture, the side door opened and out came another man. Kelly had remained calm, but Cal watched her begin to turn pale. She knew too. No longer was this about pretending to be journalists—this was about surviving a situation more dangerous than either of them previously believed. And Cal was convinced a trap was being laid for them.

Just then a booming voice from the back door called Iselda's name.

Cal spun around to see a large man standing with his arms folded outside the back door. The man's mere appearance didn't frighten him, but something else did. On his forearm were these words tattooed: La Pelona. Cal shuddered. He couldn't be sure if it was the same guy, but he knew instantly that FBI agent had lied to him. Cal knew for sure this was a trap.

Kelly and Cal followed Iselda up the back steps and into the house. He wondered if this was the last daylight he would ever see. Cal stared at the blue sky before glancing at his tormentor. Cal couldn't see the man's eyes since a dark pair of sunglasses shielded them, but he knew he was being watched. Cal stepped inside.

Mr. Hernandez greeted him immediately with an outstretched arm.

"Mr. Murphy, so pleased to make your acquaintance. Thank you so much for coming to my humble abode."

Cal smiled. There was nothing humble about Hernandez's place. The opulence oozed from every nook in the room. It screamed, "Look at me and love me." And it made Cal sick. From the marble floors to the priceless Egyptian antiques affixed to the walls, the decadence made Cal wonder how many inhumane and ruthless acts it took to earn the money to afford such riches. But he had to stop. He was here to help Noah get his son back, not judge a known cartel boss.

Cal finally spoke. "You have a very lovely home, Mr. Hernandez."

"Thank you, Mr. Murphy. Right this way, please." He ushered them down the hall to his library where Cal was to conduct the interview.

Cal and Hernandez both sat in plush chairs across from one another while Kelly knelt and stood. Even if the interview was fake, she wanted to capture a powerful portrait of one of the world's most ruthless men. It wasn't every day that these opportunities arose and Kelly wasn't going to ignore it.

Cal pulled his pen and pad along with his recorder out of his bag and prepared to begin the interview.

"Is it OK if I record this?" Cal asked. "My desire is to be as accurate as possible in using your responses in the article."

"I'm comfortable with that. Are you ready to begin?"

"I am. Are you?"

"Go ahead and start asking questions whenever you want."

Cal pushed the red button on his digital recorder and began the interview.

"So, Mr. Hernandez, let's start at the beginning. When did you first get involved with making coffee?"

Hernandez shifted in his chair before he spoke.

"Well, ten years ago, I was on a trip for pleasure in Colombia and I met this beautiful woman at a private beach resort. It turns out her father ran one of the country's most successful coffee operations. Two years later, I married her and I began to learn the family trade."

"What have you learned during that time?"

"I've learned that good coffee—like so many things in life—can't be rushed. You can't be rushed to drink it and you certainly can't be rushed to roast it. Most people make mistakes when they don't spend the time to think things through. We make impulsive decisions and what could be a great idea is worthless. So many entrepreneurs look at the coffee market and think they are going to dominate because they have a good product. But it takes more than a good product to be successful. It takes hard work. It takes determination. It takes patience. And most of all, it takes someone who is willing to roll their sleeves up and do whatever is necessary to help a dream take flight."

Cal scribbled down Hernandez's words. It actually sounded like good business advice—until Cal remembered who he was interviewing after a chilling statement.

"When someone is committed to an idea, they don't let anything stand in their way. Nothing. They do whatever is called for to see it through."

Cal couldn't be sure, but he would've sworn he saw Hernandez's nostrils flare during his previous comment.

For the next 45 minutes, Cal gathered all the information for a great profile piece on Hernandez. Kelly captured the power of Hernandez with tight portrait shots, especially when he began blowing ringlets from cigar smoke.

It was 2:20 and Hernandez was anxious to conclude the interview, as was Cal.

"So, is this everything you need?" Hernandez asked.

"I think we've got everything," Cal answered. "Kelly, do you need any more shots of Mr. Hernandez."

"Nope. I think I'm good."

"OK. It looks like we're ready to go then, Mr. Hernandez. Thank you so much for allowing us to come out and do the interview on such a short notice."

"It's not a problem," Hernandez said. "But if we had more time, I could have taken you downtown to see our roaster. That's what you get for being impulsive and not taking the time to plan for things. Just remember that Mr. Murphy: If you want to be successful, you need to plan for it.

He grabbed Cal by the arm.

"Acting impulsively will get you killed," Hernandez added.

Terror washed over Cal's face as he froze, staring at the cartel boss. He couldn't hide his fear, which was now pouring over him in waves. The look on Cal's face had to be addressed.

"Killed, as in, killed in business," Hernandez added. "You do know I was speaking metaphorically, right?"

Cal nodded on the outside but he was shaking his head on the inside. He knew Hernandez wanted him dead that instant. And since he likely knew Cal was coming, Hernandez was prepared. Cal feared they might not ever make it past the driveway alive.

Neither of them said a word.

CHAPTER 27

CAL TURNED ONTO THE QUIET TWO-LANE ROAD
and drove toward Juarez. A rocky hillside served as a barrier on
the right side of the road, while a perilous ravine invited a treacherous end on the other. He glimpsed at his rearview mirror several
times. Nothing. After a minute of driving, he exhaled and broke
the silence.

"Kelly, I think that guy near the door when we went into Hernandez's house was the same guy who tried to kill us yesterday,"
Cal said.

Kelly stared blankly at him without saying a word.

"Are you OK, Kelly?"

She broke her gaze before releasing whatever emotions she had
repressed.

"Am I OK? Am I OK?! We were just inside the home of a ruthless monster who has more money than he knows what to do with
but has decided to kidnap a little boy. He apparently has already
tried to kill us! We are in one of the most dangerous cities in the
world! And we don't know if anyone is actually watching out for
us right now! So, no! I'm not OK, Cal. I'm terrified for my life,
for your life, for that poor kid's life—and I just want out of here!"

She folded her arms and sank into her seat.

Before Cal could think of a soothing word to console her, he became distracted by the truck approaching him from behind at a rapid speed.

"What the ..."

Before Cal could issue a warning to Kelly, they both lurched forward as the truck hit them from behind.

Bam!

Kelly screamed. Cal began to lose control of the car as the jolt from behind forced him to start weaving across the road.

Smash!

Cal glanced in his mirror to see a large black truck bearing down on their car again.

"Do something, Cal!"

But his options ran short. Slam the car into the hillside and try to out run the thug? Pull the emergency brake and attempt to do a 180 on a two-lane with no margin for error? Slam on the brakes? None of his choices had safe outcomes.

"Cal! Do something!

"There's nothing I can do!"

The truck quickly pulled up next to Cal in the outer lane and forced his car off the side of the road, pinning the passenger side door against the hillside. The truck rested close enough to the car that Cal was unable to open his door. They sat their helpless.

"What are we gonna do?" Kelly asked. She frantically tried to roll down her window, but there wasn't room for her to squeeze through the opening between the car and the hill.

"I don't know, Kelly. Pray?"

Just then, a bulky man stepped in front of their car. He was carrying a sledgehammer.

"Oh, my God, Cal, we're gonna die! He's gonna beat us to death!"

Kelly's hyperventilation almost led to her passing out. Her eyes grew wild and a horrifying shock set in across her face.

Smash!

The hammer came crashing down onto the windshield as the glass splintered in a thousand directions from the point of impact.

Kelly kept screaming, only stopping to take a deep breath and scream some more.

Cal rummaged through the glove compartment and under the seats for a gun. It was an FBI vehicle, which should have a weapon somewhere. No luck.

Smash!

This time the hammer ripped through the windshield and pulled some of the glass away with it. *Two more hits and it's going to be all over.*

Cal couldn't make out the face of his attacker but he was big. He briefly considered they might have a chance since it would be two against one. But he could see the man's girth and realized speed would be their only weapon, though they couldn't get out to use it.

Smash!

The hammer pulled away almost a third of the windshield as more of the shattered glass sprinkled across the ground. Cal never thought it would end like this. Bludgeoned to death at the hands of a cartel henchman. This is why he didn't do drugs. Not only were they bad for you but they also meant you crossed paths with people like the one beating down his windshield.

Kelly was still screaming when the fourth blow to the windshield all but annihilated it. She curled up into a fetal position, covering her head with her arms. Cal thought his final act of bravery might be to give Kelly a chance to escape. He thrust himself in front of her as the man ripped the remaining block of windshield off the car.

No saving little Jake. No reuniting a boy with his parents. No leaving Mexico alive. It was all but over.

CHAPTER 28

THE FBI AGENT POSITIONED at the top of a hill overlooking the two-lane road leading to Mr. Herandez's compound didn't want to answer his phone. It was Agent Solterbeck, the mastermind of this plan. He wouldn't like what he was about to hear.

"Any sign of Cal and Kelly?"

"No, sir."

"Weren't they supposed to be back an hour ago?"

"At least. The appointment was for an hour and a half. It's four-thirty now."

"Have you seen anything else?"

"Just a few cars here and there. And a small smoke cloud."

The agent studied the winding road below. No sign of Cal and Kelly's car. In the distance was a small beat-up blue car rambling along. It was the first vehicle he'd seen on the road for the past forty-five minutes.

"A small smoke cloud?" Solterbeck asked. "Can you tell what's causing it?"

"No, but this is Mexico, sir. It could be anything. It could be a farmer setting his field on fire, a neighbor burning tires."

"I don't like this. Drive around and see if you can see anything else. They should have checked in a long time ago."

Five minutes later, the agent was driving along the two-lane road, searching for clues to Cal and Kelly's whereabouts. Two miles down the road, he turned around a bend and saw a small plume of smoke rising from the ravine. He wanted to stop and investigate, but there were several vehicles parked along the road with people trying to determine how they could help.

The agent slowed down to talk to an old man hobbling across the road.

"Que paso?" the agent asked.

The old man explained that there were two people in the car who were dead. The car was burned and the people were burned so badly that they looked all black.

About that time, a police car pulled up and an officer got out and began rambling down the embankment. That was the agent's cue to leave. He pointed his car in the opposite direction and looked down the ravine. The car wasn't recognizable any more but he could tell it was an agency-issued vehicle.

He picked up his phone and dialed Solterbeck.

"It looks like Cal and Kelly are dead," the agent said.

"What?"

"Yeah, I just left the scene. The smoke was coming from a car fire and there are two bodies burned beyond recognition. It looks like our special operatives are dead."

Solterbeck let out a string of expletives before abruptly hanging up. The plan had failed.

* * *

NOAH GREETED ELLEN AT THE AIRPORT with a kiss and a long embrace. The worst part of this ordeal was the fact that they weren't together during this time. They figured it would raise fewer questions if they were apart. More than anything, they needed to put on the appearances of normalcy to avoid suspicion.

"Have you heard anything?" she asked.

"Not today," he answered.

"So we don't know if they rescued him yet or not?"

"No. I was supposed to get a call from the FBI an hour ago, but nothing."

Just then Noah's phone buzzed. It was from an unrecognizable number.

"Noah Larson," he answered.

"Noah, this is Agent Solterbeck."

"Have you heard anything?"

"No, we haven't. And I'm afraid we have some sad news."

"Oh, no." Noah crumpled into a seat, awaiting the worst. Ellen put her arms around him as anguish washed over her face.

"Don't worry. It's not Noah."

"What is it then?"

"It's Cal and Kelly. We believed they were murdered today by Hernandez's people."

"Oh, no. That's horrible." Ellen begged to know what had happened. He mouthed that Cal and Kelly were dead. She started crying, realizing the implication of their deaths.

"Yes, I'm afraid Mr. Hernandez must have suspected they were working with us and killed them."

"So, what now? What are you going to do?"

"We're going to sit tight for now and figure out a plan to rescue your son."

"Are you kidding me? Sit tight? The Super Bowl is 48 hours away."

"I'm aware of that—and that's why we want to make sure we have the best plan possible to rescue Jake. I know this is tough, but please be patient with us. We're all working around the clock to save your son."

"OK, thanks."

"I'll be in touch."

Noah ended the call. He turned toward Ellen and hugged her again. Then they both started crying softly. Hope that they would ever see Jake alive again began to fade.

CHAPTER 29

WHEN THE SLEDGEHAMMER RIPPED into the windshield for the fourth time, Cal was expecting the worse.

Instead of reaching inside the car to jerk Cal and Kelly out, the hulking man offered his hand in assistance. "Hurry up and get out, Mr. Murphy. I need you to move quickly if you want to save that boy," he said.

Cal hesitated but then held his arm out for the man to help him. *Maybe this guy is so cruel that he wants to offer me hope before crushing me!* As soon as the man helped Cal out of the car and onto the ground, Cal thought about running. If he could find a way back to Juarez, he could escape and tell the FBI what he learned. But there was Kelly. If he ran now, who knows what this beast might do to her. Cal decided to stay put.

Kelly stopped screaming long enough to realize that the man had decent intentions despite his dramatic entrance into their vehicle. She allowed him to help her out of the car before rushing to hug Cal. They both stood and stared at the man, not sure what was going to happen next.

"I must apologize for my violent introduction, but it is necessary for your safety," the man said. "My name is Carlos Rivera and I want to help you."

The journalists said nothing. Cal noticed a handful of intimidating tattoos on Rivera's arm, but not "La Perona." His trust needed to be earned.

"I understand you might not trust me, but you have to believe me," he said.

"Why are you trying to help us?" Cal asked.

"I know this might sound crazy to you, but I want to help. I know I work for Mr. Hernandez and do many horrible things for him. I have to. I have no choice. But I also have a six-year-old son. And I no longer can sit by and watch them abuse Jake the way that they are. It's cruel. Mr. Hernandez's sense of decency is gone. He's going to kill Jake when the Super Bowl ends. He has no intention of returning him once he gets what he wants. That's how he works."

Cal took a moment to let everything sink in. His life wasn't over, but neither was his fight. Rivera actually wanted to help him.

Rivera continued.

"I know you might want to run and never come back, but you still have time to save Jake."

Cal hadn't considered leaving altogether but maybe Kelly had. However, Rivera's explanation and plea seemed to resonate with her.

"What do you want us to do?" she asked.

"My cousin is waiting at the bottom of this ravine. He will take you some place safe. Mr. Hernandez is moving Jake today and it will be much easier to rescue him at that location. Tomorrow, attend the Saturday morning mass at San Augustín Chapel and speak with Padre Francisco. He will tell you what to do next."

Cal peered across the street and into the ravine. Large boulders clung to the steep incline.

"Are you sure this is safe?" Cal asked.

"Anything is safer than Mr. Hernandez knowing you're alive," Rivera said.

Cal and Kelly looked at each other and prepared to cross the road.

"Wait, before you go, I need your wallets, passports, cell

phones, everything," Rivera said.

"How are we going to contact anyone?" Cal asked.

"You won't. And it's best that you don't for now. I'm going to make it look like I caught you and killed you. It's the only way to keep you safe for now."

Cal and Kelly fished everything out of their pockets and handed them to Rivera.

"Now go. You need to hurry."

* * *

RIVERA WATCHED THE JOURNALISTS run toward the ravine, descending out of sight. He walked to the back of his truck and pulled a tarp back across the bed. Beneath it lay the dead bodies of a man and a woman. Rivera had no idea who they were. Two people who got in the way of something Mr. Hernandez wanted to do, he suspected. They had been in the walk-in cooler for three days and Hernandez had asked him to bury the bodies earlier in the day. He decided against it. Planting their bodies in Cal and Kelly's car would confirm his story.

He loaded the bodies into the car, buckling them into place. Rivera inserted the man into the driver's seat and the woman in the passenger's side. He stuffed the pockets of the dead bodies with Cal and Kelly's belongings. Before finishing his masterpiece, Rivera beat on the side of the car with his sledgehammer a few more times for good measure. He then put the car in neutral and pushed it toward the rocky ravine. It rolled about 50 yards down the ravine until coming to rest against a large boulder.

Rivera scrambled down the rocks toward the car. Armed with a gas can, a lighter and a few strips of old rags, he prepared to finish the job. He doused the vehicle with gasoline, taking extra precaution to ensure that the bodies were soaked. After circling the car to make sure he was ready, he inserted the rags into the gas tank. He lit the inside of the car on fire before lighting the rags. Then he ran.

He was halfway back up the ravine before he heard the first explosion. Kneeling for cover against a boulder, he looked back down to see flames engulfing the car. Surely someone from the house would have seen the explosion. They would assume Rivera completed his special assignment.

CHAPTER 30

CAL AND KELLY REACHED THE BOTTOM of the ravine in time to see their car explode against the clear afternoon sky. They were supposed to be in that car, probably dead long before it went up in flames. And if they wanted to live, they hoped other people would believe they were inside it. But they weren't. The game wasn't over. People's lives were still at stake. There was no time to mull over the danger they had just escaped.

They both looked at each other with knowing glances. Somehow they were still alive.

"It gets worse before it gets better, right, Cal?" Kelly said.

"Remind me to enroll for photography classes when I get back, OK?"

Kelly smiled, breaking a half hour of tension.

They began walking along the dusty road, waiting for their mystery chauffeur to appear.

"Look, I know you feel bad about this and that you're to blame for dragging me into all this, but I'm here because I want to be," Kelly said.

Cal didn't look up.

"I never should have brought you here."

"You didn't, Cal. You asked me to come because you needed help. And I came because I wanted to help you and help a little boy get back to his parents. You don't need to feel guilty."

"I can't help it. Back there ..." Cal paused. Tears welled up in his eyes. "Back there, I don't know what I would have done if he tried to kill you first. I felt helpless."

"Cal, you acted on your instincts. You protected me. I won't forget that."

"But I didn't do anything. If he wanted to kill us, I couldn't have protected you."

"Well, maybe you should enroll in some karate classes and leave the photography to me."

Cal cracked his first smile since earlier that morning. He adored Kelly's witty one-liners.

She turned serious again. "I know I freaked out back there, but we're going to do this. We're going to get that boy back with his parents where he belongs. We have to."

Cal was still processing everything when a banged-up Ford Festiva pulled up next to them.

"Cal? Kelly?" the driver asked.

"Yeah. That's us," Cal said.

"My cousin, Carlos, told me you would be waiting for me here. Please get inside the car."

They both got in the back seat as requested.

"My name is Josuel. It's nice to meet you."

Josuel's English was sufficient though Cal could tell any prolonged conversation would likely be a struggle.

"Where are we going, Josuel?" Cal asked.

"I have a friend who is going to let you stay with him for a few days. He will be... how do you say... discreet?"

"Discreet?"

"Ah, yes, discreet."

And that was the end of the small talk. Josuel pulled back onto the two-lane road that Cal and Kelly had used to access Mr. Hernandez's compound.

"You might want to hide under the blanket I put in the back," Josuel said.

"Why is that?" Cal asked.

"This is a very watched road. It would not be good for either of us if we are seen together."

Cal and Kelly didn't say another word as they slipped beneath the blanket.

* * *

AFTER 20 MINUTES THE CAR came to a stop.

"It's safe to come out now," Josuel said.

Cal and Kelly climbed from beneath the blanket and sat up. They were inside what looked like an auto repair shop. Two cars were up on makeshift blocks, while another car rested on the ground with no wheels.

"What is this place?" Cal asked.

"It's where I work. There is a couch and a chair in the office where you can stay tonight."

"Is this safe?" Kelly asked.

"For tonight. We are closed on the weekends. No one will look for you here."

"Where are we exactly?" Cal questioned.

"We are two blocks northeast from the square where your hotel was located."

Josuel proceeded to give them instructions on how to get out, how to lock up, and what to do if anyone came around.

"Do you need anything else?"

"I guess not," Cal said.

He lied. He needed a fresh change of clothes and a hot shower. He needed to be out of Juarez and back in Houston writing about the Super Bowl. He needed this nightmare to be over.

Josuel lingered waiting for an official dismissal.

"We'll be fine," Kelly said, giving Josuel permission to leave. "Thank you again."

"It was my pleasure," he said before opening the garage door and pulling out.

Cal yanked on the chain to close the garage door. Through two small windows near the top of the 20-foot ceiling, the afternoon sun dimly lit the interior. Cal searched for lights inside the cramped office as he thought about their instructions for the next day. A small lamp sat on the corner of the worn wooden desk, awash in a sea of paperwork. Cal clicked it on and the uncovered bulb flickered to life.

"What do we do now?" Kelly asked.

"I think we ought to let our FBI handler know we're alive," Cal answered.

"But we don't have a cell phone."

"Well, there is a phone here. I memorized the emergency number."

"Look at you, Boy Scout. Always prepared."

"I didn't take this assignment lightly—and I'm sure glad I didn't now."

Cal picked up the phone on the desk and dialed the number.

"Please enter your security password," came the automated response on the other end.

Cal punched in the numbers on the keypad and waited. A series of clicks and whirls passed the seconds while Cal awaited the voice of a real human being.

"Is this Mr. Murphy?" asked the voice on the other end.

"Yes, it is. I'd like to speak to Agent Solterbeck."

"Hold on a minute."

He looked at Kelly, who stared at him anxiously awaiting any crumb of news he might toss her way. A few more clicks and then another voice.

"Cal Murphy? Is that you?"

"Sure is. I just wanted to let you know that we're still alive and working on rescuing Jake."

"Oh, thank God you're alive. One of my operatives called in to report that you had been killed in a fiery explosion off a road near Hernandez's compound."

"Well, that's what we were hoping everyone would think."

"What happened?"

"Well, Hernandez was on to us. I knew we were in trouble when I saw that tattoo I told you about on the arms of one of his bodyguards. We were able to identify where they are holding Jake."

"Oh, that's great. We need to get that information from you as soon as possible so we can act on it."

"Unfortunately, it's worthless now."

"What do you mean?"

"Well, after we left, we were run off the road by one of Hernandez's men. He told us he would help us save Jake but he had to make it look like we were dead."

"He must have done a pretty good job. They found bodies on the scene with your identification cards."

"I don't know what he did, but he sent us down a ravine to meet with someone who picked us up and brought us to this auto repair shop."

"Do you know where you're at? We can come get you right now."

"We do know where we're at, but we still want to help. This guy who helped us today—his name was Carlos Rivera—gave us instructions on how we can meet up with some people tomorrow who will give us the information we need to safely get Jake back."

"So you want to play this thing out?"

"Yeah, if that's OK with you. Kelly and I both know the risks involved. We figure if we've come this far, we should go all the way to make sure Jake gets home safe."

"It's up to you. We can have a team there in ten minutes to take you back home."

"No, I think we'd rather stay and get that information for you. We do need our personal belongings from our room and a new cell phone. Do you think you can put them in a backpack and leave them at San Augustín Chapel for us tomorrow morning?"

"We'll see what we can do."

"Thanks."

"Good luck, Cal. We'll look forward to hearing from you."

Cal hung up and relayed the conversation to Kelly. They were worn out from running for their lives and masquerading around the home of a cartel boss. At least he thought they were dead. At least they could sleep in peace for a night.

* * *

MORALES USED A NEW BURNER PHONE to take another picture of Jake. He sent the photo to Noah Larson along with another message:

we know you told … your son will pay

It was not a pretty picture. Jake had a few scratches and cuts on him. He didn't look emaciated, but it certainly looked like someone had been bullying him.

Morales then kicked Jake, shoving him toward the door. Jake whimpered. "Stop it," he whined. It was obvious Jake was getting tired of being pushed around. But Morales didn't care. He hated babysitting the kid and had no qualms about expressing his displeasure.

"I want my mommy and daddy," Jake said.

"Shut up, kid, and get in the van," Morales snapped.

Jake stumbled forward, falling down and hitting his head on one of the cobblestones protruding out of the road. A small stream of blood trickled down his face. He began crying.

"Tomorrow can't get here soon enough," Morales grumbled.

Morales yanked the kid off the ground with one hand, being careful not to spill the liquor bottle in his other. He slammed the door shut and sped off toward the city.

CHAPTER 31

CAL WOKE UP EARLY SATURDAY MORNING feeling like he needed a shower. After all, he was going to church. He hadn't attended a church service in several years. And for good reason. He hated sitting down for an hour and being told how to live his life. He didn't need any priest's suggestions. He was doing just fine on his own. But not today. Cal was excited to go. Though he would be reluctant to admit it, he *wanted* some help now. He *needed* some intervention, like the kind he received the day before when death had darkened his soul's doorstep. It took a wild and convoluted turn of events for Cal to realize that he didn't care about the awards or the spotlight—he just wanted to get Jake home to his dad.

Kelly remained asleep on the small couch in the office. Cal rumbled around the shop until he found a large sink. It wasn't a shower but it would have to suffice. He found a relatively clean washcloth and splashed water on his face. The water chilled him. Hot water was a luxury that did not exist in Josuel's shop. The quiet time alone gave Cal a chance to prepare mentally for the day's coming events. This was it. He was finally going to do what he came here to do. It was all going to work out. He could feel it.

Cal tried to clean the dirty spots on his shirt with a rag. Scaling down an incline the day before wasn't exactly the best way to keep his clothes suitable for church. But he didn't dwell on it—and he didn't care. If people looked down on his attire, he wouldn't let it bother him. He wasn't there to impress anyone, especially complete strangers. He was there to find out how he could save a little boy.

Kelly stirred on the couch. She sat up, disoriented and curious as to where Cal was.

"Cal? Cal?" she called.

Cal half jogged back to the office to assure her that everything was fine.

"Yeah, Kelly? I'm here."

"Oh, I forgot where I was."

Kelly's hair was matted to her face and Cal had yet to see her eyes through the tangled mess. She brushed her hair aside with her hands and looked around. She tried to open her eyes wide and yawned. It was the first time Cal had seen Kelly so unfiltered in the morning. He found her routine endearing.

"You ready for today?" he asked.

"I will be," she said, yawning again. "Is there a shower in this place?"

"Eight o'clock in the morning and your sense of humor is wide awake."

"Seriously, Cal, is there a shower here?"

"Come on, Kelly. This is a repair shop in Juarez, Mexico. What do you think?"

"I don't know."

"It's early and what I do know is that you'll have to be content with cold water from a large sink and a semi-clean rag to wash up with."

"Is there any coffee?"

Cal knew she was out of it, but he thought she might be joking. The wry smile creeping across her face gave it away.

"We've got some time, but we need to be at the church at nine o'clock. Do you think you can be ready by then?"

Kelly stood up. "After all this time, do you really still think I'm a dainty little princess who can't face the world without doing my hair and nails and smearing makeup all over my face?" She lightly stomped her foot for effect.

Cal didn't say a word. He simply smiled at her.

"Well, do you?" she demanded.

"No, Kelly, I don't."

"OK, good. I just had to make sure. Sometimes I don't know about you."

Kelly woke up in a feisty mood and Cal just wanted to stay out of her way. Maybe she was like this every morning. Maybe she needed her coffee. Maybe she was upset about being in Mexico and not enjoying Super Bowl parties. Cal couldn't be sure, but he knew silence was the best way to inoculate himself from her mini-rants.

Cal found an old Spanish soccer magazine in the bottom of the desk drawer beneath two half-empty bottles of Jose Cuervo. After spending the next 30 minutes trying to read the magazine and avoiding Kelly altogether, Cal finally spoke.

"You ready to go?"

"Yeah. Let's get out of here."

They exited the shop and stepped into the bright sun. The day was young but Cal knew time was running out for Jake.

* * *

NOAH FELT RELIEVED after he hung up the phone.

"What is it?" Ellen asked.

Noah grinned but said nothing.

"Did they find Jake?" she asked again.

"No, but Cal and Kelly are still alive."

"What? How did that happen?"

"Apparently, they faked their own death to escape and are supposed to get the FBI his exact location today so they can rescue him."

"Oh, thank God! Please, just get my little boy back to me!"

Noah felt the same way, but he didn't verbalize it. He could feel the pressure beginning to mount upon him with each passing hour that Jake remained captive. While he held out hope that the FBI would be able to rescue Jake, it wasn't a foregone conclusion. And if Jake wasn't around by the time the game started, he was willing to throw the game. It's not how he wanted to end his career, but nothing was more important to him than seeing his son alive.

CHAPTER 32

CAL AND KELLY STEPPED into the church ten minutes before the 9 a.m. mass was to begin. Cal wasn't sure if they would stand out or if anyone would notice them. They were supposed to be dead, and he certainly didn't want anyone who worked for Hernandez to think otherwise. Attempting to keep their profile low, Cal led Kelly to sit in the back corner of the room next to the three confessionals. If something went wrong, Cal figured that might be a good place to hide.

Although Cal wasn't sure what to expect, he preferred to get the information from the Padre and go save Jake. He could skip the homily. No such luck.

"Buenas días, Padre," Cal said as the priest approached along the outer aisle.

Padre Francisco stopped at the last aisle and spoke softly.

"Buenas dias. Do you have something you would like to confess after mass?"

Cal looked at the priest and nodded.

The priest also nodded and continued walking down the aisle.

"Looks like we're here for the duration," Cal said to Kelly.

Kelly wasn't listening. She was too busy scanning the church for any suspicious parishioners, perhaps someone she noticed yesterday at Hernandez's place from the previous day.

Cal joined her and saw nothing that alarmed him.

"I don't see anyone I notice," she said in a hushed voice.

"Neither do I."

Just then the organ music began and everybody stood up. Moments later they sat down again. Then everyone kneeled. Cal was lost. So was Kelly. Their decision to sit in the back was a good one if they were trying to be inconspicuous. Mimicking the up and down movements of the others in the congregation was much easier to do from behind.

The priest's homily was about never losing faith in God. His homily covered a story from the New Testament where Jesus raised a girl from the dead. A man asked Jesus to heal his daughter because she was sick and dying, but Jesus took his time and the girl died before he arrived. Jesus then brought her back to life.

Padre Francisco reached the crescendo of his homily: "Everyone has seen a little child recover from illness, but to see someone raised from the dead? Our faith is built the strongest when we see God do the impossible in our lives."

Cal's mind drifted off, thinking about his situation. If he didn't know any better, he would've thought the priest was speaking directly to him, trying to sway him from his cynicism. Cal knew he tipped his feelings about God with his question the day before. But he brushed off the idea. The situation wasn't impossible. In fact, it was simple. The priest tells him where to find Jake. Cal calls the FBI. Jake reunites with his parents. The Super Bowl is played fix-free. Everyone is happy. No God necessary.

Cal then looked at Kelly, who appeared to be listening intently. She had professed her disdain for organized religion to him before, but she was paying close attention, even nodding in agreement at some of the things Padre Francisco said. Maybe this ordeal was getting to her. Cal dismissed it and anxiously awaited the end of the service.

* * *

A FEW PARISHONERS GREETED Padre Francisco as they filed out. Cal and Kelly stood up but went nowhere, as they waited for the priest. After a few moments, he shuffled to the confessional and sat down. Cal joined him.

Cal said nothing and waited for the priest to speak.

"Son, the answers you seek can be found in the book of San Juan 1:50. You may also find some help in verse 39. Be blessed."

Cal committed the scripture references to memory and then got up.

"What did he say, Cal?" Kelly asked.

"Do you have a Bible?"

"No."

"Grab one of those and let's go," Cal said, pointing to a small stack of Bibles near the exit of the church.

"I'm not stealing a Bible. Are you crazy?"

"OK, let's look these up."

Cal was amused at the contents from the first verse the priest gave him, though he wasn't convinced that was the relevant portion.

"San Juan one fifty? San Juan one fifty? I've seen that somewhere before."

"Where? Do you remember?"

"Uh, yes. It was in the brief the FBI gave me on Hernandez. I think that's an address for Hernandez's roasting plant. We crossed Avenida de San Juan on our way to the hotel. I don't think it's that far from here."

"And what does the other verse mean?"

"It refers to four o'clock in the afternoon. So, I'm guessing something is happening at Avenida de San Juan at four o'clock. Let's go."

Cal looked back across sanctuary. Padre Francisco stood watching them in the now vacated chapel.

"God be with you, my son," he said.

Cal nodded and led Kelly out into the street. He respected the priest's beliefs even if he didn't share them. Cal still felt like he could do this on his own with Kelly. But if the priest thought he needed God's help, what could it hurt?

They headed for the Avenida de San Juan.

CHAPTER 33

CAL AND KELLY WALKED TWO BLOCKS before either of them uttered a word. Kelly broke the silence.

"Don't you think we should call the FBI now? It's time to let them handle everything, right?"

"Almost," Cal said. "I want to check out the address first. I could be wrong about it."

"OK, fine. And then we call the FBI. I'm ready to get out of here and let the professionals do their job."

"Agreed."

After walking two more blocks, they arrived at Avenida de San Juan. If there was a roastery nearby, it wasn't in use. The scent of diesel and rotting garbage overpowered any aroma of coffee beans, if there even were any. Approximately a hundred yards away was a building with the address from the cryptic message given to them by the priest. The white stucco building looked like a storage facility of some type, definitely not a roastery. Opaque square windows flanked a large roll-up door. A small door on the near corner of the building appeared to be the only other way inside.

Cal and Kelly scouted out the quiet street. An elderly man pushing a wooden cart, pedaling floor mats and processed pastries was the only person on the street.

"This looks like a great place to hide your drugs and weapons," Cal said.

Kelly agreed. "No kidding. This place is quiet. Or maybe they keep it this way."

"Let's get a look inside and then I'm calling Solterbeck."

Cal and Kelly crossed the street, checking to see if any new people had wandered onto Avenida de San Juan. They hadn't. Only the squeaking wheel of the old man's cart and a few distant car horns interrupted the eerie silence.

Cal approached the door and jiggled the handle. It was open. He turned back to Kelly and winked at her before slipping inside. Kelly followed him.

The inside of the room was vast and appeared mostly empty. The ceiling stretched three stories high and was vacant with the exception of a catwalk that hung between the wooden trusses. Several storage containers were double stacked on their right as they walked forward. The concrete floor was swept clean. A faint smell of coffee beans permeated the air, but the smell of gunpowder was stronger. As they walked deeper into the building, Cal saw a row of machines that looked like they were used to make bullets. He caught the glare from several casings resting on top of the machines.

Just as Cal quickened his pace in an effort to inspect the machines, Kelly screamed. He stopped and spun around to see her holding her hand over her mouth and pointing. Rivera's body hung from the ceiling.

"Noooooo!" Cal screamed, abandoning all sense of secrecy.

"Cal, we've got to get out of here," Kelly said.

Bam!

The door slammed shut. Cal and Kelly spun toward the entrance to see the looming shadow of Diaz.

* * *

RICKY LONGSHORE HAD BEEN WAITING patiently to hear

from Agent Anderson at the FBI. The feds instructed to keep the line open and be alert for any more unusual activity. It had been a quiet week, all things considered.

But Saturday morning, another suspicious bet appeared. It wasn't unusual for people to place large sums of money on the underdog. But extraordinarily high amounts from new bettors always made Longshore uneasy. The relative anonymity afforded people at The Oasis made this easy to do, especially when they placed the bet in cash.

Longshore called a few of his friends at other sports books to see if anyone had placed suspect bets in the last 24 hours. Nothing. It was business as usual. But Longshore was convinced that maybe there was something else at play, maybe someone else had knowledge of the fix. He couldn't be sure, but the man who placed the suspicious bet was staying in one of the suites at The Oasis. It would be easy to keep track of him if anything else about him seemed suspect.

CHAPTER 34

"YOU'RE NOT GOING ANYWHERE," Diaz said. He walked slowly toward the journalists. "There's only one way to get out of here alive—and that's with me."

Cal placed his hands in the air as an act of surrender. He had already run from this beast once before and barely escaped. His chances of a repeat performance with Kelly in tow weren't nearly as good among the unfamiliar streets of Juarez. Kelly followed Cal's lead and did the same. Cal glanced once more at Rivera's body dangling from the rafters and winced.

"This way," Diaz said, pointing toward the door with his gun.

They walked through the door and were greeted by two more of Hernandez's men. The men shoved Cal and Kelly into a van that was parked curbside on the still-quiet street.

Diaz followed them, keeping his gun pointed at them.

"Mr. Hernandez found out you were working with Rivera by trying to fake your deaths. Mr. Hernandez doesn't like employees who aren't loyal," Diaz said. He paused. Then he finished his thought. "You should have minded your own business."

Cal didn't like being talked down to either, especially by a meathead who made his living by torturing and terrorizing others. He glanced at Kelly, who was watching Cal intently.

"It gets worse before it gets better, right?" she said.

"Shut up! No more talking!" Diaz growled.

Diaz then took two handkerchiefs and blindfolded his two prisoners. It was all for show. Once Cal and Kelly took them off, they would know where they were.

After three minutes, the van stopped abruptly. Cal could hear the van door sliding open. He felt Diaz's beefy paws grab his arm and yank him out of the van and onto the ground. Cal tumbled out and felt Kelly do the same.

"Get up, you two!" Diaz yelled. "I have a special surprise for you!"

The two men helped Diaz hustle Cal and Kelly through a door. Once inside, Diaz ripped the blindfolds off of them, revealing a familiar environment: the auto repair shop.

Josuel was the first person they saw. He grinned at both of them.

"Hola," he said.

Cal lunged at him before Diaz constrained him.

"What kind of cousin are you? Doesn't family mean anything to you?" Cal said, glaring at Josuel.

"Family means everything to me. Carlos was related to me on my mother's side of the family through marriage. But Mr. Hernandez is my father's uncle. What do you say in the USA? 'Blood is thicker than water'?" Josuel laughed and then sucker punched Cal, who staggered back before falling down.

"Don't you ever talk to me like that again?! Do you understand, gringo?"

Grimacing, Cal looked up at Josuel and slowly nodded.

Cal got back up to his feet and looked around. That's when he noticed Jake sitting in the office, watching a small television that wasn't there before.

"Tie them up with the kid," Diaz said.

One of Hernandez's men marched Cal and Kelly into the office. Jake, entranced by the television, didn't look up. Once the ropes were secured, the man locked the three hostages into the office and left. Cal watched Diaz discussing something with his underlings. There was no question who was in charge.

Cal turned to Kelly. She looked tired and beaten. The emotional ups and downs were taking their toll on her.

"Kelly, I know this has been rough, but I need you to pay close attention. You need to memorize this number and password in case we get separated. Do you understand?"

She didn't answer his question.

"What are you going to do? Cal, don't do anything crazy!" she begged.

"Look, I don't know what's going to happen, but this is important OK. Memorize this and don't forget it."

Cal went over the numbers and the password with Kelly. It would get her to their FBI handler, who could arrange an extraction if necessary. Once he was satisfied that she knew the numbers, Cal thought it might be a good idea to build some trust with Jake.

"Hey, Jake, I'm Cal Murphy and this is Kelly Mendoza. Your dad and mom are really worried about you."

Jake hadn't moved since they entered the office, staring at the television.

"We're going to get you out of here, OK?"

Jake turned and looked at Cal. There was a three-inch cut on Jake's right cheek that Cal hadn't noticed when he first looked at him.

"Are you OK? Have they been treating you well?"

Jake turned back toward the television, still in a trance.

"I know you've been through a lot recently, but we're going to do our best to get you out of here."

Jake said nothing, leaving only the silly sound effects from the cartoon he was watching to fill the dead air.

Cal looked at Kelly. "He's been through a lot obviously."

He tried once more.

"Look, Jake. I know you don't know us and you may not want to trust us, but we want to help you get back with your mom and dad. If we run, I want you to run too and stay with us, OK?"

Still no response. Cal would have to trust that Jake heard, understood, and would comply when the time came. Otherwise, it would all be for naught.

* * *

SOLTERBECK WAS GROWING CONCERNED. He should have heard from Cal and Kelly by now. It was getting late in the afternoon and still no word.

Then his phone rang.

"Sir, I'm patching through a call to you. They requested to speak specifically to you," said the FBI dispatcher.

"Who is it?"

"He wouldn't say, sir. Here he is."

"Solterbeck."

"Mr. Solterbeck, we need to make a trade."

"Who is this?"

"Who I am is not important. Who I want you to release from your custody is. I want you to release a prisoner by the name of Hector Gonzalez. He's serving a sentence in Pollock. You'll do exactly as I say if you want to see two certain American journalists alive again."

"We don't negotiate with terrorists."

"That's a lie and you know it. But neither am I a terrorist. I'm more of an opportunist."

"We want the kid, too."

"The kid? My offer only involves two journalists—a Mr. Murphy and a Ms. Mendoza. I will exchange them for Hector at ten o'clock tomorrow morning at the following coordinates."

Solterbeck took down the coordinates without saying a word.

"See you there, Agent Solterbeck."

The line went dead. Solterbeck slammed his phone down. He picked his cell phone up and texted his team to be at the office within an hour for an emergency meeting.

He then dialed the number for the U.S. penitentiary in Pollock. He already had a plan.

CHAPTER 36

RICKY LONGSHORE WANDERED down the hallway to the
security suite to check in on his mystery guest. A bank of high
definition screens blanketed the far wall as well as the near wall to
his right. Three Oasis security agents watched the screen with in-
tense interest. Two of the agents were drinking coffees from Star-
bucks while the other was draining a Red Bull without taking his
eyes off the screen.

"You guys still have eyes on our mystery guest?" Longshore
asked.

"You mean, Dick Nixon?" one of the agents asked, chuckling.
He pointed to the screen so Longshore could watch. The man
was wearing a Dolphins' jersey, jeans, a Dolphins' cap and sunglasses. He also had a full dark beard.

"Is that what he checked in under?"

"Yep. Paid for his room in cash."

"For what he lacks in originality of a pseudonym, he certainly
makes up for in mystery. What has he been doing today?"

"Oh, nothing exciting. He's played a couple of games at the
blackjack tables. But no booze or girls, if that's what you mean."

"He hasn't been to my sports book again, so I was just wondering if he's some high roller. But apparently not, eh?"

"Looks like a small time gambler to me."

"OK, keep me posted if he does anything else suspicious."

Longshore reached for the doorknob to leave the room before one of his agents shouted excitedly.

"Look, his beard just fell off," he said pointing at the screen.

Near the entrance of a bathroom, the guest was fumbling for his beard. He kept his head down, but nobody around him seemed to notice.

"Zoom in closer," said one of the other agents now leaning closer toward to the screen. "I know who that is!"

* * *

SOLTERBECK'S OFFICE BUZZED with activity ninety minutes later. Agents scurried about, generating reports and gathering information about location of the swap. Operatives talked on the phone, coordinating efforts with agents on the ground in Juarez. Solterbeck secured permission to release Gonzalez and have him transported by plane to Briggs Army Airfield in El Paso.

Solterbeck's cell phone buzzed. It was the FBI's deputy director, Vance Williams.

"What's going on down there, Solterbeck? I thought you were supposed to get this situation under control. Get the kid back. Save the Super Bowl. We're all happy. But not only have you accomplished squat, you're now releasing a man convicted of killing eight federal agents!"

Solterbeck anticipated this call and repeated the lines he had rehearsed.

"Sir, we're trying to make lemonade out of lemons here. It looks bad but I think I have an idea about how we can come up with a resolution that makes everyone happy."

"I doubt there's any scenario where releasing a cartel hit man is going to make everyone happy."

"You'd be surprised, sir."

"Well, I better be surprised tomorrow or else you're going to be looking at another assignment. You got that?"

"Loud and clear, sir. I'll update you when I have some news."
The director hung up.

Solterbeck buried his head in his hands. If he was honest with himself, it did look bad. Every move he had made so far had been an epic failure. He knew he never should have let Cal and Kelly go. He knew Hernandez was on to them when images of Diaz appeared in photos taken from traffic cams. Diaz had spent the last six years on the FBI's most wanted list. For as bad as Gonzalez was, Diaz was worse. Fourteen dead federal agents over the past six years. Border patrolmen. FBI agents. He was even suspected of killing a CIA agent on vacation in Cancun just for sport. Diaz stabbed the man to death and chopped his head off, leaving it on the bed for his wife to find when she came back from the pool. He was a monster.

But there was no time to second-guess his decisions. Now he had to make one good one, the kind that would save people's lives; the kind that would save his job; the kind that would cross the line.

CHAPTER 36

CAL GREW TIRED OF SITTING locked in the tiny office. Kelly slept splayed across the couch, while he sat on one of the couch arms. Jake just stared at the television. Hour after hour of cartoons rolled by on the screen. They seemed like mindless short stories with no real moral. The protagonist was likeable; the antagonist was cruel. The antagonist would almost win and then— *BAM!*—the protagonist would hit his archrival on the head and escape. If only it were that simple.

Any attempt at hitting Igor over the head would result in getting slapped around. And slapped hard. Maybe even a few cuts. The end result wouldn't be pretty. This wasn't a cartoon. This was real life, and Cal needed a real good idea.

* * *

AT SEVEN O'CLOCK, a shift change brought a fresh guard to the repair shop to watch over Hernandez's three prisoners. Cal had seen the man at Hernandez's compound. It was Morales.

Morales tapped on the window. Jake looked up and Morales waved at him. Jake's physical reaction to the sight of Morales made Cal wonder what exactly happened between the two. Jake curled up in a fetal position and started sucking his thumb. Cal tried not to imagine the worst, but something bad had happened between them. That much was evident.

Fumbling with his keys, Morales eventually unlocked the door and slid a bag of burritos into the room along with three water bottles. He then locked the door behind him and sat outside.

Cal ripped open the bag and pulled out a burrito. He offered one to Jake, who continued to pretend like Cal didn't exist. He decided against waking Kelly. She looked too peaceful and appeared as though she could use the extra rest. Cal scarfed down his portion and thought about his plan.

Another hour went by before Kelly stirred from her nap. Her burrito was cold, but she didn't seem to care. Cal waited a few minutes until she was awake before he started to share his plan with her.

"I think it just might work," she said.

* * *

IT WAS 10:30 p.m. and Cal watched Morales stumbling around the shop, clinging to a bottle of tequila. It was almost empty. Cal watched the scene unfold as he hoped it would. Morales look at the remaining swig in the bottle and swirled it around. It wasn't even 11 p.m. on a Saturday and he would be all out of liquor without a chance at a refill until the morning.

The loud clanging noise startled Jake. He sat up, still half asleep, and looked traumatized. Morales began overturning tool boxes and pushing over chairs, upset about something.

"Don't hit me! Don't hit me!" Jake screamed.

Cal rushed to his chair and knelt down next to him.

"Hey, it's OK big guy. Nobody is going to hit you. You're with us now. We're going to keep you safe," Cal said, rubbing Jake's head to reassure him.

Cal tucked a blanket back around Jake and told him to go back to sleep. He then moved to the couch.

"I don't even want to think about what this monster did to

Jake," Cal whispered.

"Yeah. Whatever it was, it must've been bad for him to react like that," Kelly said.

"It looks like it might be time to put our plan into action."

Cal reached for the desk drawer where he had seen two bottles of Jose Cuervo. He pulled out one of them and tapped on the glass to get Morales' attention. Morales ran straight for the office and began pulling out his keys. He struggled to get them in the lock. He was already well on his way to being drunk; Cal hoped to get him get all the way there.

Once Morales got the door open, he snatched the bottle from Cal's hand.

"I guess you're good for something, gringo." He then head-butted Cal. He snarled at Kelly before shaking Jake and screaming to wake him.

Jake awoke again, startled at the sight of his tormentor.

Morales cackled at the fear he wrought on his captives. Then he slammed the door shut, causing a picture to fall off the far wall.

"Are you sure getting him more drunk is a good idea, Cal?" Kelly asked, tucking Jake back underneath his blanket.

"Just give it some time. And be ready when I give you the word."

An hour passed and Morales' motor skills continued to diminish. He stumbled around the shop, slamming into things. He punched car doors and slurred threats at no one in particular. He even missed his mouth a couple of times while trying to take another drink. He was almost done with the bottle of tequila when he started staring at it like he did the previous one.

Cal shook Kelly, who had been resting.

"It's almost time," he said. "Get ready."

Kelly scooped up Jake in her arms. He didn't resist, content to remain asleep. Cal marveled at Kelly's natural ability to nurture. Though Cal was protective of her, he didn't consider her as fragile. Kelly suspected everyone thought she was fragile when they did things for her, but Cal simply tried to act like a gentleman. Sometimes that meant protecting her. And if she felt that meant he thought she was fragile, Cal didn't care. But he thought of her more as a rugged, do-it-yourself kind of woman. He had never seen her treat someone so tenderly.

Cal turned his attention back toward the shop where Morales was stumbling around. It was time.

Cal tapped the glass and waved yet another bottle of tequila. This time, Morales lumbered toward him, banging into large objects scattered about the room. Two cars and a large toolbox took the brunt of Morales' wrecking ball approach to walking. He finally arrived at the door and unlocked it.

Morales stood in the doorway and stuck out his hand for the bottle.

"Gracias, señor," he said, slurring his words.

Instead of handing Morales the bottle, Cal swung it with all his might, knocking Morales in the head. Morales staggered back and fell onto the ground. Kelly scooped Jake up and headed toward the office door.

"Go! Go! Go!" Cal yelled, putting himself between Kelly and Morales.

Once Kelly cleared the doorway and headed toward the shop exit, Cal began to run after her. Before he could take a second step, he felt a huge hand wrap around his ankle with a death grip.

"Run, Kelly, run!" Cal yelled as he struggled to get free.

Cal's efforts to escape failed. Morales' grip was too strong, sending Cal tumbling to the ground. Morales dragged Cal's body toward him before pinning him down with his knee.

Morales began berating Cal in Spanish while punching him repeatedly in the face. He was so disheveled that he seemed resigned to let Kelly and Jake escape. Instead, he was going to take out his anger on Cal.

* * *

SOLTERBECK'S CELL PHONE BUZZED. It was the FBI

answering service.

"Agent Solterbeck, I have a call coming through from Kelly Mendoza. She said it's urgent and that she needs to speak to you."

"Yes, let me talk to her."

The line clicked in.

"Kelly? Are you OK?" Solterbeck asked.

"Yes, I am. I've got Jake and he's fine. But Cal didn't get away," she said. Solterbeck could tell she was out of breath.

"Where are you?"

"I don't know. I'm in Juarez somewhere near our hotel."

"OK, just get me the cross streets and we'll have one of our agents come pick you up in 10 minutes. Just sit tight and stay out of sight."

Kelly gave Solterbeck the cross street names and awaited the extraction team.

CHAPTER 37

NOAH LARSON REMAINED RESTLESS in his bed. He would've been this nervous if it was just the Super Bowl. But this was *the* Super Bowl—and he was going to make sure the Seahawks lost. His restless sleep kept Ellen up as well.

"I think I'm going to throw up," Noah announced. "I just can't do this any more. I can't keep lying to everyone and pretending like it's all OK because it isn't. Our son could die because I'm the quarterback of a football team and some greedy bastards are trying to get rich quick."

Ellen allowed her emotions to follow Noah's. As long as he was calm, she was calm. But when he became unhinged, it was a toxic combination. She started sobbing.

"I can't believe I went along with this and didn't tell anyone. I feel like such a fraud."

Just then, Noah's phone buzzed. It was Solterbeck.

"What?!" Noah said excitedly. "Are you serious?"

Ellen waited breathlessly for Noah to get off the phone and tell him the good news that she wanted to hear.

"What is it, Noah?"

"They've got Jake! He's safe and will be here in the morning!"

Noah and Ellen hugged each other tightly, crying tears of joy together. Jake was coming home.

* * *

BY ONE O'CLOCK in the morning, Cal began to wonder how he would function the next day. The drunken beast had beaten him long and hard. A nice shiner and some nasty body bruises resulted from Morales' tequila rage. He even suspected he had a broken pinky finger on his left. But Cal couldn't be too upset. It was his idea to get Morales drunk enough to escape. Cal just couldn't finish the escape part. This was the price for not completing the plan. But he was still alive.

Morales kicked Cal around for forty-five minutes before calling in reinforcements. He wanted to make sure dawn didn't break without having at least one hostage. If he were empty handed, Hernandez would surely kill him. But with Cal alive, death was not quite as certain.

Cal lay face down on the concrete floor, right where Morales had left him. Without the strength to attempt an escape, Cal didn't move. Hernandez had some sort of plan for him. Why not just stay alive and live to see another day? Cal knew when it was time to retreat—and this was it. He eventually fell asleep.

CHAPTER 38

CAL AWOKE TO THE SOUND of a garage door rolling up and the shouting of men's voices. His neck was stiff and his back sore from sleeping on the concrete floor. He moved slowly but quickened the pace when one of Hernandez's men shoved the point of an assault rifle into his back.

"Move, amigo!" the man barked.

Cal got up and shuffled in the direction the man with the gun was prodding him. Another man blindfolded Cal before shoving him into the waiting van. Cal couldn't be sure what time it was, but what did it matter? He was on someone else's schedule right now, doing whatever they told him to do. Maybe he would get out of this alive, maybe he wouldn't. And while something like time was irrelevant in his situation, just knowing it brought back some sense of normalcy.

"What time is it?" Cal asked, hoping someone in the van would answer him.

Silence.

"Does anyone know what time it is?" he asked again.

Nothing.

Maybe it's the language barrier. He tried it in Spanish. "Que hora es?"

"*Es hora de que te calles,*" came the response. It was followed by a whack to his head with the butt of a rifle. Not exactly the answer Cal was hoping for, but it didn't hurt too much to ask.

Cal couldn't see through the blindfold, but he felt like he was seated in the back of the van. It was the same one Hernandez's men had brought him here in. Hernandez customized the van, making it perfect for operations such as these. Long seats ran around the inside perimeter, replacing the bench seats. The floorboard didn't feel slick; the metal had been covered by a spongey substance. *Probably to absorb all the blood*, Cal thought.

After a few more minutes of men shouting and screaming instructions in Spanish, Cal heard the garage door crash down before the van door slammed shut. The van lurched forward, speeding off in an unknown direction.

Cal had no idea what to expect, but he hoped they wouldn't dump his body off a cliff. This was not the way he wanted to end it all, a footnote on the inside page of a newspaper or buried on a website somewhere. He wanted his life to matter.

* * *

SOLTERBECK STEPPED OUT OF THE HELICOPTER at the site Hernandez gave him. He nursed his scalding cup of coffee. The morning light peeked over the horizon for the first time that day. Instead of being here, Solterbeck would have preferred to be asleep in his own bed. But this situation dictated he have a second plan and a third plan. The location was remote without multiple ways in or out—for most people. However, with access to plenty of FBI resources on this case, he made sure numerous options existed. Solterbeck needed Cal out of there alive. It would be good for his career and good press for the agency, a win-win situation that everyone could feel good about.

The coordinates Solterbeck received were at the top of a bluff. A winding dirt road led to a precise location as the only manageable way in or out by car. The surrounding area was extra sandy with large boulders. Navigating a vehicle through that area would present a challenge to even the best of drivers. However, it was the bluff's unique shape that formed almost a peninsula, making it perfect for a swap. Hernandez's men would take the position closest to the exit while Solterbeck would have to wait. It was a type of extra insurance. The nearby ridge overlooking the bluff also gave Hernandez the opportunity to position long-range snipers to make sure everything went smoothly. This concerned Solterbeck, but he knew the location would be far from ideal from his perspective.

Solterbeck jumped onto the helicopter and left after 20 minutes of scouting the area. He would be back in less than three hours for the swap. He had a few phone calls to make.

* * *

THE VAN CARRYING CAL bumped along toward its destination. He still had no idea when he would arrive or what would happen after he got there. He just knew they weren't getting there soon enough. While Cal wouldn't consider himself fluent in Spanish, he knew enough so he could pass the time by listening to the conversation buzzing around the van. The men guarding Cal didn't seem to think he could understand much of what they were saying. Their tongues wagged loose and free.

Cal gathered a few important details. First, Hernandez wasn't there nor would he be coming. Secondly, Hernandez needed some type of insurance. Cal wasn't sure what that meant or what it was referring to, but he had a good idea that they weren't talking about the kind you can buy to protect your home, life or vehicle.

Suddenly, the terrain switched from pavement to dirt. The potholes, however, jolted the van with the same frequency. But wherever they were, it wasn't near Juarez any more—or on well-traveled stretch of the highway.

The van turned sharply left, flinging Cal to the right. One of the men shoved Cal back to his original seat. More potholes and sand. A minute later, the van skidded to a stop. Hernandez's men hustled Cal to the opening of the van before removing his blindfold. The door slid open and Cal squinted at the morning sun beaming down.

Cal needed a few moments for his eyes to fully adjust. The men forced Cal out of the van. Cal staggered forward. He was standing on the edge of a cliff.

CHAPTER 39

A LIGHT RAIN THRUMED against the bay window overlooking the tarmac at George Bush International airport. Noah fidgeted with his hands, rapidly bouncing his knee. Ellen adjusted her oversized sunglasses. The thick clouds blanketing the Houston sky didn't warrant shades, but they did serve to hide the mascara streaking down her face.

This wasn't the week Noah expected six days ago. He wished he could have it all back, enjoying a crowning achievement in his career with his teammates and family. *The Super Bowl.* Noah had worked his whole life to get to this point, the penultimate goal for every football player. Yet here he was, less than 10 hours before kickoff and all he could think about was his family.

The airport granted the Larsons use of a private room that connected to the tarmac. It would be the quickest way to see Jake once he arrived. The minutes dripped by. Would he ever arrive?

Finally, Jake walked through the door. He sprinted straight for Noah, who met him halfway. Noah scooped up his son and spun him around. Jake didn't say a word. He just buried his head into his dad's shoulder and sobbed.

Noah never thought the Super Bowl could seem so small and insignificant. Today, it did. Now, he would play his final game with integrity, with his chin up. He wasn't prepared, but he didn't care.

It didn't matter. Not today. The game itself didn't *really* matter.

What mattered to Noah was the four-foot nothing, 55-pound boy who clung to his neck, feet interlocked behind his back. And his wife who sandwiched Jake with him. Nothing stopped the tears. Fear roared and hope roared back. The Larsons were all together. One last game and that was it. They would get on with the business of being a family.

Noah walked over to one of the FBI agents to inquire about Cal's status.

"I need to thank Cal," Noah said.

"Well, that won't be possible."

"He's not dead, is he?"

"No. Not yet anyway."

"What do you mean?"

"We can't really divulge that information Mr. Larson, but let's just say this operation did not go as planned."

"But he's still alive?"

"For the time being. We'll let you know something if and when we can."

"Fair enough," Noah said. He wasn't used to being told he couldn't know something. But it would have to do. Cal had to make it back alive.

CHAPTER 40

DIAZ STEPPED IN FRONT OF CAL. He was the only thing between Cal and a long fall to the bottom of a ravine.

"Hey, let's not be so hasty," Cal said. "Maybe I could be of some benefit to you and your boss."

Diaz laughed. "You think Hernandez is the boss?" he asked.

Cal said nothing. That's what he had been led to believe. Was someone else really in charge? Could it be Diaz?

"Hernandez is a hired man, a pawn doing the dirty work of someone else. He's foolish. He only does things for money. But sometimes, he gets lucky. While he's off making sure we get paid, I do the dirty work."

"Look, I can just walk away and we can forget this all happened," Cal protested.

"No, we can't," Diaz said.

He then grabbed Cal's shoulder and marched him around the corner of the van so he could see what was really happening.

Three black SUVs faced Cal's direction. He noticed that his van wasn't the only one in the entourage. There were four others. It looked as if the whole Hernandez clan had joined them, expecting some sort of shootout. Cal noticed a man near the other SUVs was wearing a bullet proof vest and an FBI hat.

Before Cal could figure out what was happening, Diaz explained.

"We already have a plan for you, Mr. Murphy. We are trading you for Hector Gonzalez, Hernandez's best, how do you say it, 'fix-it' man?"

Diaz then picked up his phone and began dialing. He didn't exchange any pleasantries—strictly business.

* * *

SOLTERBECK ANSWERED HIS PHONE. It was Hernandez.

"The terms have changed," Hernandez announced. "We will trade Cal Murphy for Hector Gonzalez. No one else."

"What's the matter? Can't keep your men sober enough to guard a woman and a six-year-old boy?" Solterbeck asked.

"We can always rescind our offer, perhaps establish different terms."

"Well, we got what we came for. If you decide to keep Cal hostage, we're not going to spend many resources fighting it. He's pretty much worthless to us—and worthless to you if we aren't willing to give you anything for him. So talk tough with me. Show me your machismo. I don't care. You either take it or leave it. This deal is going away forever if you don't take it."

Hernandez was quiet.

"We still on?" Solterbeck asked.

"Yes. Show us the prisoner."

Solterbeck motioned to his men to show Hector Gonzalez to Hernadez's men. They removed a sack over his head and waited. Solterbeck could see a trio of men using binoculars to confirm that it was indeed Hector. After a few moments of silence, Solterbeck heard a voice speak.

"OK, we'll show you Mr. Murphy."

In a similar fashion, Solterbeck's personnel were positioned around the area. They attempted to confirm Cal's identity. Once they agreed it was him, they nodded affirmingly at Solterbeck.

"Let's make the switch," Solterbeck said. "Let's send them out at the same time."

* * *

WHEN HERNANDEZ WASN'T AROUND, Diaz took charge. He carried out his boss's wishes with effortless efficiency. Boss wanted a man dead? Diaz took care of it. Boss wanted someone tortured for information? Diaz leapt at the opportunity. Hernandez's level of trust with Diaz approached blood-relative level. And this morning, Hernandez needed his top soldier's loyalty more than ever.

Diaz grabbed a fistful of Cal's shirt and shoved him toward the federal agents waiting for the exchange to occur.

"Just keep walking, gringo," Diaz said.

Diaz watched Cal walk toward the FBI agents positioned about 75 yards away. Diaz also watched Hector begin walking toward him. The swap was going as planned.

Bang! Bang! Bang!

The rifle shots echoed in the canyon below before Diaz realized what happened. Hector collapsed to the ground.

A gunfight erupted between Hernandez's men and the FBI.

Diaz yelled at Cal. "Stay down or I'll take you out myself!"

Then Diaz crawled army style side-by-side with his prized hostage until they reached the van.

* * *

CAL WAS NOT ACCUSTOMED to such chaos. Action in the newsroom on election night or after covering a marquee sporting event created a hive of activity. But it was forgettable compared to this. Whizzing bullets. Double-crossing criminals. Dying people. Cal watched deadly ammunition bore into the dusty ground all around him. He wanted to burrow in after them and hide until this blood bath ended. Sooner or later one of those bullets was going to find him—and then what? Cal tried not to think about what it would feel like to get shot, but he knew it couldn't be a pleasant experience. *I don't want to die!*

The best thing Cal had going for him was that he was Diaz's only collateral, the only way he could make a deal and get out of this situation. But someone pulled the trigger too early. Someone shot Diaz's defenseless friend. Someone ruined Cal's morning.

The shoot out lasted no more than two minutes, but it felt longer to Cal. He lay on the ground for a few moments, paralyzed by fear. Then Diaz shoved him into the van. Cal curled up in the fetal position and took advantage of the steel-plated van's armored exterior.

As soon as the gunfire stopped, four men loaded into the van and it sped away without another shot fired. Cal didn't care what was happening as long as everyone stopped shooting. He eventually mustered the courage to peek outside the van and saw the FBI's tactical team watching the van leave without firing a shot. *They let Diaz and his crew escape?* The van bumped along the dirt road for about five minutes, making a handful of turns.

Suddenly, the van skidded before slamming into a pair of SUVs, halting the entourage. Cal tumbled near the front of the van and looked through the front windshield to see a half dozen men begin to spray the van with bullets using automatic weapons. He scrambled behind the driver's seat and hugged the floorboard. The windshield shattered as the assailants riddled the van. Cal looked toward the back of the van and watched his captors heads and chests explode in a bloody mess before they could even fire a shot in the right direction. Dead bodies slumped all around him.

Cal didn't move. He didn't want anyone to check the bodies and discover him still alive. Who knows what they might do to him? He didn't breathe. Not until he heard the voices of a few men shouting in Spanish, car doors slamming, and the tires kicking up dust.

Then Cal freaked.

"Oh, my God! Oh, my God! I'm still alive!"

Cal patted down his chest and thighs, looking for a bullet wound. Maybe he would have felt a bullet rip through his skin or maybe not. At the moment, his adrenaline coarsed so fiercely through his body he felt like he could've accomplished any un-fathomable feat. His search for a bullet proved futile. He was alive, unscathed.

Instinctively, Cal grabbed a handgun off one of the dead guards. He needed to get out of the van and get some place safe. Who knew if the attackers were coming back? Maybe they wanted some trophies or needed a head to hang from the overpass.

Cal tucked the gun behind his back and crept up toward the front. He needed to see if there was anyone nearby. There wasn't. He exited through the sliding door and crouched down as he walked. The prisoner had been shot from long range and who knew if someone still had a scope on the van. If there was ever a time to be cautious, this was it.

As Cal peered around the corner of the van, he saw nothing familiar. Just more vast Mexico wasteland. More dusty desert. More canyon in the distance. A lone tree on the horizon and two roads leading in opposite direction to nowhere. Cal decided to start walking in the direction the van was pointed. It was obviously the way out. His mind felt jumbled from the chaos. *Just walk.*

Cal ambled along the lonely road. He would have preferred to get off the road, perhaps walk in the ditch or disappear in the nearby woods. He didn't want to be seen in the open. But there was nowhere to hide. Vast nothingness. If this was his day to die, only a cruel God would let him survive everything he had experienced in the past day or so only to be killed while walking along a dirt road. But maybe his part was done. Maybe the priest was right and God had used Cal—and now Cal's time was up, his good deed done. But before Cal could plumb the depths of his own soul and contemplate his mortality and place in this world, he heard the roar of several car engines.

Cal whirled around to see three black SUV's speeding toward him, causing a small dust storm behind them. Instead of running, Cal chose to stand firm. Maybe the SUVs could give him a ride.

Then Cal recognized the SUVs. He exhaled in relief. It was the FBI.

CHAPTER 41

"YOU ALL RIGHT?" SOLTERBECK asked Cal.

Cal didn't answer, staring down the road and toward the canyon.

"Look, that's not how it was supposed to go down."

Cal remained silent, his shock turning to anger.

"I know you're stunned about what just happened and you could've very easily died today. But you didn't. Someone was looking out for you, Cal."

Finally, Cal spoke. "Yeah, well I know that someone wasn't you. I could've died because one of your trigger happy agents decided to gun down the prisoner I was being swapped for."

"That's not what happened."

"Oh, really? Then help me understand why you were raining down bullets on these men knowing full well I was with them."

"Something went wrong, but we were careful not to shoot you."

"Please, spare me. I wasn't born yesterday. You got lucky you didn't kill me—and you know it. You probably thought I was a ghost walking down the road."

"Things aren't always as they seem."

"Well, it seemed like you were doing your best to get me killed, not really trade for my life."

"Look, the truth is nobody on my team took the shot that killed the prisoner we were trading."

"Then who did?"

"Someone from a rival cartel."

"You mean to tell me another cartel found out about this swap and just happened to show up?"

"They found out because we told them."

"You told them?"

"Yes, we didn't want word getting out that we would trade hostages for a cartel's assassin in U.S. custody. So, we tipped off a rival cartel. One of their snipers obviously couldn't wait to take him down. He murdered a lot of people. You understand that, right?"

"So you invited them to the exchange?"

"Well, we told them when and where this trade was taking place and that if they wanted to ambush Hernandez and his men, this would be a great opportunity to do it."

"Only problem is, Hernandez wasn't there."

"Yeah, we realized that once we stopped and ID'd the bodies. Do you know where he is?"

One of the FBI agents wandered over to check Cal for any possible injuries.

"I'm not sure. But Diaz told me something interesting."

"Oh? What's that?"

"He said that someone hired Hernandez to do this."

"Did you find out anything else?"

"I learned that Hernandez has an insurance plan. Not sure what that means, but that's what one of the guys said."

"He was probably referring to you."

"I don't think so. It seemed like he was talking about someone else."

"I haven't heard reports of anything else happening."

"Well, how's Kelly and Jake? Are they OK?"

"Yeah. They're fine. Jake is already back with Noah. Everything there is great."

"Good. And they weren't hurt?"

"Nope. A few scratches but nothing to speak of."

"Thank goodness."

"Look, I'm really sorry about today, Cal. I know you're upset. But you're alive. I appreciate all you've done this week to help get Jake back to his family. You'd make a great candidate for the FBI, you know?"

Cal didn't say anything. He stared off into the distance, still seething over another monumental government screw up that by some complete miracle didn't result in him getting killed.

The FBI agent finished inspecting Cal and released him. "He looks good to me."

Cal finally spoke. "There were a few moments where I wasn't sure I was going to make it. But I did, no thanks to you."

"Again, I'm sorry, but I'm glad you're alive and well. We still have a few more questions for you back at our office before we get you home."

Cal paused. "Look, I don't mean to be a pain, but I really want to get back to Houston. I want to feel normal again, and I think the Super Bowl will help me do that. Can I answer your questions tomorrow?"

Solterbeck thought for a minute before relenting. "OK."

Cal heard a helicopter in the distance. It belonged to the FBI.

Cal was going to the Super Bowl.

CHAPTER 42

CAL CHECKED HIS WATCH as he waited for the FBI plane. Thanks to the helicopter tranport, he arrived at Biggs Army Airfield at noon, five and a half hours before kickoff. Figuring in the 90-minute flight to Houston and the estimated two hours it would take him to get to his hotel and get cleaned up, Cal figured he might make it to the game with an hour to spare. Maybe it would be enough time to wander onto the field during warm-ups and say hello to Noah. Maybe.

The events of the past two days shook Cal. He started to think about the way he could've died—gunshot to the head, run off the road and down into a canyon, beaten to death, thrown off a cliff, gunned down by masked assailants. But none of those things happened. Somehow, he fended off the knocks of the grim reaper. He refused to answer, denying the grave its pleasure. And while Cal's desire to witness the Super Bowl felt superficial in the light of everything that happened, he needed to feel normal again, like this was just some bad dream. He needed to talk to Kelly.

"Can I borrow your phone?" Cal asked Solterbeck.

Solterbeck handed Cal his phone without saying a word.

Cal dialed Kelly's number.

"Hello?" she asked.

"Kelly, it's me. I wanted to let you know I'm OK."

"Oh, Cal. I didn't know what was going to happen to you. Someone from the FBI called me earlier and told me you were OK. I've been dying to talk to you."

"Let's try to use some other metaphor, OK?"

Kelly laughed. "Sorry. I know it's a bit sensitive right now."

"You're telling me."

"So what really happened after Jake and I escaped?"

"Well, I didn't. Hernandez tried to trade me for one of his assassins with the FBI."

"Are you kidding me?"

"No. I wish I was."

"So that's how you got free?"

"Sort of. The FBI agreed to exchange me for the assassin, but then everything went wrong."

"What happened?"

"According to the FBI, some rival cartel's sniper shot the assassin during the exchange. One of Herandez's men pulled me back and started a gunfight with the FBI. Then Hernandez's men thought the FBI was trying to pull one over on them, I guess. So Hernandez's men decided to keep me since I was their leverage, but a few miles down the road the rival cartel ambushed us. They killed everyone but me."

"Whoa! Why do you think they let you live?"

"I think it's because they thought I was dead. I pretended to be dead when they looked inside the van and they drove off. Eventually, the FBI picked me up."

"That's messed up, but I'm so glad you're OK, Cal."

"Me, too. It's great just to hear your voice. What did you do after you escaped with Jake?"

"Well, I called that number you made me memorize and I got someone at the FBI to pick us up."

"What was Jake like?"

"Scared. He hardly said a word. But I could tell he felt safe."

"You did a good thing, Kelly. Making sure that kid got home to his mom and dad safely—he'll remember you for the rest of his life."

"I'm not the only one he'll remember."

"Yeah, well, we can only hope it doesn't damage the kid psychologically for the rest of his life."

"No kidding."

"So, are you still going to the game?"

"I wouldn't miss it. You going to make it back in time?"

"I hope so. I've got to get cleaned up at the hotel, but I plan to be there before it kicks off."

"Be safe, Cal, and I'm glad you're OK."

"Thanks. You too. I'll call you later tonight."

Cal hung up. He glanced at the television, already two hours into the six-hour pregame coverage of the Super Bowl. *How long does it take to breakdown one football game?* Cal thought.

Airing on the television was a feature about the quarterbacks and a comparison between the two. Cal always thought comparing quarterbacks was the dumbest statistic ever reported by sports writers and sports broacasters. *They are never even on the field at the same time!* It was like trying to determine who was better: an English teacher or a History teacher. They both taught different subjects and would naturally go about their teaching differently— just like quarterbacks facing different opponents would go about their business differently. But every red-blooded American sports fan likes to compare things and rank who is better. Cal hated this practice since even the use of statistics are subjectively employed in determining who is the best.

In the comparison story, Noah looked calm and relaxed on the screen. *This had to be filmed before this week.* Noah laughed as he recalled a story from playing youth football as a ten year old that started his legend in Beaumont, Texas. He threw a pass that was batted into the air, which he caught and then ran 50 yards for a touchdown. Throwing a touchdown pass to himself paled in comparison to the success he had in college at the University of Texas. He led the Longhorns to a national title, willing the team to victory in a championship game that went into triple overtime. The music in the background sounded heroic. It was the story of

Noah's football accomplishments—and his crowning achievement was within his grasp.

Then the story shifted to Miami's star quarterback, Hunter Newton. Undersized and underappreciated his whole life, Newton didn't get any of the chances afforded to Noah. No big college scholarship offers. Newton starred at a junior college before a football factory in the South offered him a scholarship. He took it and made the most of it. Six years later, he had the Dolphins in the Super Bowl. The piece cast Newton as a player who never got any credit for his team's good fortunes. In college, Murray State had two running backs rush for over a thousand yards. Newton just handed off to them. The reporter interviewed Newton's dad as well, as he told stories of how no one ever thought his son was good enough. But Newton always proved them wrong. Once Newton made the Dolphins' roster, he thought all the criticism would go away—but it didn't. No one ever seemed to give the guy credit.

Cal smiled. The feature story pitted two sides against each other in classic sports journalism style: good vs. evil. Entitled quarterback vs. gritty, hard-working quarterback. But Cal knew the truth. Noah was the reason Seahawks were in the Super Bowl. The Dolphins were there because of their defense, not Newton. Everybody knew it. But the feature story tried to make you think there was some hidden drama. Nobody who knew anything about football would buy it.

He stopped mulling over the piece he had just watched when he heard his name called.

"Cal ... Cal!" Solterbeck said.

Solterbeck handed Cal his bag.

"Cal, I can't thank you enough for all you did. I'm really sorry everything went down like it did. That wasn't supposed to happen."

"I know," said Cal, taking his bag. "But everything worked out, right?"

"Thankfully, it did. Let me know if you want any official FBI comments for that award-winning article you're going to write."

"Will do. And thanks for getting me back for the game."

"Well, unfortunately, there have been some delays. The plane won't get here for another three hours."

"Are you serious?"

"Yeah, I'm sorry about that. Nothing I can do about it at this point."

Cal sighed and then huffed. *You'd think after all I did, someone could get me to the game!*

He slumped in his chair, forcing himself to watch more meaningless pre-game Super Bowl coverage.

CHAPTER 43

NOAH LARSON STOOD IN THE TUNNEL with tears in his eyes. He knew everyone would be able to see, but he didn't care. Maybe the announcers would use this as an opportunity to talk about his reputation as a soft quarterback. Or maybe they would use the visual as proof that the aging veteran's dream of playing in the Super Bowl had come true. But they would be wrong.

Noah teared up because his family was safe. Some greedy people almost took one of the most precious things in his life for money. It made him sick. He had dreamed his whole life of playing in this game, walking out of the tunnel at this exact moment. He used to think this was what it was all about. But he had worshipped a lie. Difficult times have a funny way of revealing who we really are and what we really value. And Noah realized he didn't value this. The Super Bowl. Being a sports hero. None of that mattered at all. In the greater context of life, it meant nothing. But Ellen and Jake? They were everything. He couldn't wait to spend the rest of his life with them. No more practices. No more interviews. No more demands.

His tears said good-bye to a life he once revered and hello to what mattered most to him.

But even through his blurred vision, nothing clouded his final goal: winning the Super Bowl. He knew if he played his best, it would happen. Nothing would stop him. He would make Seattle throw another parade—the best one the city had ever seen—and then he would disappear.

"Starting at quarterback for the Seattle Seahawks, number ten, Noah Larson."

The voice over the public address system echoed in Reliant Stadium as he ran through the fog and onto the field. Cheerleaders shook their pom-poms. The crowd roared. Highlights played on the jumbotron. His name flashed on the matrix boards.

Noah met his teammates along the sideline at midfield. The testosterone in the team huddle could have powered the state of Rhode Island for a week. It was time to kick off.

Noah took his place on the sideline for the kickoff as Zombie Nation's "Kernkraft 400" pumped through the speakers. The stadium swayed. Flashbulbs popped. The game had begun.

* * *

CAL GREW AGITATED over the fact that the game had kicked off and he wasn't there to see it.

"I can't believe the FBI has a private jet that doesn't have a television in it," Cal grumbled.

"We do," said one of his accompanying agents. "Just not this one."

Cal sighed in disgust.

"We do have wireless internet. You could probably listen to the game on your smart phone."

"Yeah, that'd be great—if I had it. Some kid stole it while I was in Juarez."

"Here use mine," the agent said, handing Cal his phone.

Cal thanked him and took his phone.

"Not a sports fan?"

"Oh, I am. But I like the Raiders. It's been a while since I've cared about the Super Bowl."

Cal laughed as he searched for an app to follow the game. He found one and began listening.

Larson drops back to pass. He's got Hayes wide open on the far sideline. Hayes makes the catch at the 40. He makes a move. 35, 30, 25. One man to beat. Hayes with the stiff arm and he's going to take it in for a touchdown. A 55-yard touchdown pass from Larson to Hayes and the Seahawks have the lead.

Cal smiled and pumped his fist in a reserved fashion.

One of the agents looked at him and smiled back. "Did somebody score?"

"Yeah, the Seahawks did on a long touchdown pass."

"Nice."

Brandon Gomez on for the extra point. The kick is up and … it's wide right! The hold looked good, but Gomez hooked it. But the Seahawks still lead 6-0 with 3:15 to go in the first quarter.

Cal shook his head. The Seahawks had only missed two extra points all year. This was not the time for Gomez to get the yips. But at least Noah Larson seemed sharp.

Listening intently to the game, Cal imagined each scene painted by the announcer. Nothing happened for the next several minutes in the game as the teams traded punts. Then the Dolphins scored on a 20-yard touchdown run midway through the second quarter to take a 7-6 lead.

Cal felt the sweat start to bead up on his forehead. He was supposed to be unbiased, an objective observer, a reporter being the eyes and ears for people in the most watched and listened to game of the year. But this was his team, the Seahawks. Outside of Steve Largent and Cortez Kennedy, Seattle didn't have a history of great players. Plenty of great players wrapped up their careers with the Seahawks, but they didn't start and finish there. They epitomized milk toast. Some success but nothing to make people take notice.

And that's why Noah Larson leading the team to the Super Bowl held special meaning for Seahawks fans. Larson was drafted by the Seahawks and had played his entire career there; a man determed to win a title for the franchise and city. It was a quest ten years in the making.

So despite everything he had been taught about remaining objective, Cal just couldn't. He wanted the Seahawks to win more than anything. He wanted it as a fan. He wanted it as a sports writer. This was the kind of story he wanted to write about. And in an unlikely way, Cal played a big role in making sure they actually had a chance to win. Cal thought about his extended family and what a big deal a Super Bowl win would mean to them. They all toiled with this team through both the good and the bad. They had their hearts broken before. But it was going to be different this time. This time, the Seahawks were going to win. At least that's what Cal wrote before the game. Maybe it was his professional opinion; maybe it wasn't. No one would know. Picking the Super Bowl winner was never easy and if he was wrong, none of his readers would complain.

As the plane began to descend, Cal lost his wi-fi connection. He handed the phone back to the agent and prepared for the landing.

Cal's stomach was in knots. The Seahawks were playing in the Super Bowl and he was in a private jet. Get me out of here and to the stadium! Cal clamped his hands down on the arm rest. The game frayed his nerves more than landing did. He couldn't wait to leap from his seat and begin listening to the game again.

The tires barked as the plane made contact with the tarmac. Cal let out a sigh of relief as the nose tilted down to a safe position and the plane slowed to a creep.

Once the plane stopped, Cal thanked the pilots and the rest of the agents on board and sprinted toward the stairway leading him to ground transportation. He needed a cab and fast.

Instead of his normal game of people watching, Cal focused on a single goal: getting in a car and back to his hotel and then to the game before it was over. He still needed to look somewhat presentable. A fresh shower would help him feel better, not to mention make him socially acceptable again. The stench emanating from his body was beginning to bother even him.

Curbside at the airport, Cal flagged down a cab driver. He decided to keep his small bag with him instead of putting it in the trunk.

The cab driver spoken broken English. Cal couldn't place his accent exactly, but he guessed it was somewhere in Eastern Europe.

"Are you from Bosnia?" Cal asked.

"Close. Moldova," he replied. His accent may have been broken but he understood Cal just fine.

"What's the score?" Cal asked, immediately recognizing the familiar radio announcer's voice as he slid into the backseat.

"14-13, Dolphins," the driver answered.

Cal sighed but said nothing.

"Missing an extra point? That's a disgrace!"

The cabbie's comment shocked Cal. He struck Cal as more of a soccer fan, not American football.

"Do you know how much time is left?" Cal asked.

"It's halftime."

Down by a point at halftime. The Seahawks could still pull out a win. *At least I don't have to endure Brittany singing at halftime.*

The cab driver turned the radio up and Brittany wailed out her auto-tuned lyrics to "Toxic."

Cal moaned. He figured he would be at the stadium in time for the fourth quarter.

CHAPTER 44

"ARE YOU SURE THAT'S HIM?" Longshore asked, pointing at the mystery guest now engrossed in the game as the second half kicked off.

"No doubt about it," replied the security agent.

"Well, there's no crime in what he's done, but the whole thing makes me nervous."

"People mortgage their homes when they sense a sure bet. He's not the first insane gambler to walk through the casino doors."

"Yeah, but there's no such thing as a sure bet."

"Tell that to NBA fans."

"This is the NFL and everything doesn't always go as planned. What could make him so certain the Dolphins are going to win?"

"Maybe he knew about the fix?"

"No way. Not him. Why would he get mixed up in all this?"

"Why not? If there's a fix on, it's easy money. There's your sure bet."

Longshore couldn't fathom the idea proffered by one of his security agents. Nothing really surprised him in this business any more. Gambling brings out the worst in people in the worst way. People throw their hard-earned money into the wind—or worse, someone else's hard-earned money.

But this idea surprised him.

* * *

CAL ARRIVED AT HIS HOTEL in downtown Houston just in time to see the start of the second half. He shed his clothes and took a quick shower. Under normal circumstances, Cal would have lingered in the steamy shower and contemplated the events of the last 48 hours in great detail. But he didn't have time for that. Besides, what more was there to think about? They rescued Jake. Noah was going to win the Super Bowl. And Cal wanted to be there to see it. He wanted to soak up the atmosphere at Reliant Stadium before writing his masterpiece. At the moment, doing that meant foregoing his usual contemplative shower.

He toweled off and stared at the television. Moments later, he jumped up in the air as Seattle made an interception. Cal then danced a little jig that looked like a cross between a rain dance and a man walking across hot coals. Fortunately, no one was around to see it.

Cal pulled out his bag and dug through it for a pair of clean clothes. But he stopped. There was a letter in his bag.

"*Cal*" was scrawled across the front of the envelope.

Who would have left me a note?

Cal ripped the envelope open, scrambling to unfold the paper and read its contents. *Who knew where I was staying?* The letter was simple:

> Cal,
> Do something good.
> Room 552 Hilton Americas
> Deuteronomy 24:7
> *Padre Ramirez*

Do something good? What else was there to do? He had saved Jake. Hernandez's men were dead, his operation crippled. What was left?

Cal's hands trembled as opened the bottom dresser drawer to discover a Bible. Deuteronomy 24:7? Sounds like some all-night biblical diner.

It had been a while, but Cal remembered how to look up Bible verse references. He read it aloud:

If a man is caught kidnapping one of his brother Israelites and treats him as a slave or sells him, the kidnapper must die. You must purge the evil from among you.

OK. It's a final judgment. Vicious, perhaps. Or maybe it's justice. It wasn't what Cal expected from the priest, a man of enormous grace. Maybe Cal was reading too much into it. Surely the priest wasn't suggesting killing the man. Or was he? Whatever he meant, what did he expect Cal to do about it?

Then there was the address. What was going on in that hotel room? Was that the insurance policy?

Then Cal made sense of the cryptic note: Hernandez had kidnapped another player's child. But who? There wasn't time to guess who it was.

Call the FBI. Give them the information. Go to the Super Bowl. That was standard protocol in this situation. But there wasn't enough time. His old mission was re-assigned again: Save the kid.

* * *

HERNANDEZ TURNED HIS CELL PHONE off and slung it onto the bed. He was worried: Diaz wasn't answering. Hernandez hated the dirty work. That's why he hired men like Diaz, men with no conscience, men who worshipped money just a little bit more than he did. It's how he wielded his power. Money meant power, just not always control. And right now, Hernandez's money and power proved meaningless in his mercenary efforts to guarantee the outcome of the Super Bowl. Now he had to do the dirty work himself.

Hernandez looked at the kid, gagged and tied to the executive business chair in the corner. He exerted no effort to keep the kid quiet and sneak him into the hotel. Threaten a kid's mother if he does anything to draw attention to himself and you usually get one compliant child. But no need to take any chances now. Not at this point. It would all be over in an hour or so. The Dolphins win, Hernandez makes his millions—and the boy goes back to his family. He also makes his boss very happy. Not that he was afraid of the man who hired him, but there was no need to sully his reputation with a botched job. The only thing more powerful than money was fear.

He turned the television up and watched the game. It was too close for Hernandez to relax. Without the help of the quarterback, Hernandez's insurance plan wasn't perfect. In fact, it was far from it. But it didn't have to be perfect—just adequate. Yet with the game's score so tight, it might have been more perfect than Hernandez ever imagined.

"Third down and one from the Seattle 20-yard line. You get the feeling the Dolphins aren't going to be satisfied with a field goal here, Tim."

"Absolutely not! This is the Super Bowl and here's their chance to take command of this football game."

"Newton in the shotgun. He takes the snap. Nobody's open. He's scrambling to the outside. He gets a block on the outside. He's got the first down and more. One man to beat. Newton with the spin move and he's going to put it in the end zone. Touchdown Dolphins! With the extra point, the Dolphins are going to take a 21-13 lead late in the third quarter. Oh, man, who would've ever guessed this upset in the making? This might be one of the biggest upsets in the history of the Super Bowl!"

Hernandez smiled. Not much longer and this would all be over.

CHAPTER 45

CAL'S PHONE RANG. It was Kelly.

"Hey, Cal. Are you here yet?" she asked.

"No. Something's come up."

"What do you mean?"

"I mean, it's not over yet. I got a tip that Hernandez is possibly holding another player's child ransom."

"Who?"

"I don't know. But I'm going to find out right now."

"Are you going alone?"

"I have to. There's no way the FBI could get there in time."

"Are you sure? Have you called them?"

"I'm about to, but there's only 12 minutes left in the game."

Kelly said something but Cal couldn't make it out over the roar of the crowd.

"What did you say?"

Kelly shouted. "Touchdown, Seahawks! It's 21-20. We can win this thing!"

"I'm about to go make sure it can actually happen."

"Call the FBI to back you up. And be careful, Cal."

"I will."

Cal hung up the phone and headed out the door.

* * *

THE WALK FROM the Four Seasons to the Hilton was two blocks southeast on Dallas Street. Cal's pace quickened the farther he walked. He wanted to run but didn't want any unnecessary attention, even though the streets remained empty. Though it wasn't two marquee names from the NFL, the Super Bowl had turned out to be a good game and everybody kept watching. They would all be watching a sham if Cal didn't intervene.

Cal called one of his contacts at the FBI and gave them the address and what he suspected was happening. They said they would assemble a swat team but they wouldn't be there for another thirty minutes. Cal agreed not to go in until they arrived. He lied and said he wouldn't. Then he used the rest of the walk to formulate a plan.

* * *

HERNANDEZ WAS LOSING HIS MIND. Ten minutes left in the game and the Dolphins were clinging to a one-point lead. All this work would be for nothing if the Seahawks won. He'd even lost some men over this job. How many? He couldn't be sure. But he lost some good ones, even some he had to kill himself.

He grabbed his phone and scrambled across the room to take a picture of the boy. Hernandez jammed the barrel of his pistol into the boy's head. The boy closed his eyes and winced. He screamed as he braced for the gun to fire. It didn't. The only click he heard was that of Hernandez's camera phone, snapping a photo. The boy gasped a sigh of relief.

Hernandez fired off a text message with the photo attached to the boy's mother. He wanted to make sure the family understood he wasn't kidding about killing their son.

If someone inflicted pain upon him, Hernandez would return the favor.

Guaranteed.

CHAPTER 46

CAL'S SENSE OF URGENCY INCREASED his clarity of
thought and made him more efficient. Under normal circumstances, Cal would approach this situation differently. There
would be smiles to flash and hands to shake. He would convince
a few people that they needed to help him and give him information that was vital to revealing the truth. But that wasn't a luxury
now. Politeness didn't matter. Maybe ethics didn't either. Or the
law. The only thing that did matter was saving that kid.

As Cal approached the Hilton, he sought out the service entrance. He needed to start there to launch his plan.

He immediately located the kitchen. He found a member of the
hotel's wait staff willing to deliver a meal to Room 552. At first,
the young man balked. How could he get away with taking a random meal to the room? And then how would he explain what
happened to the paying customer's meal? Cal had an answer for
everything. All it took were the right answers—and a $100 tip out
of the FBI stipened he had been given—to convince the young
man to do it.

Cal took the stairs, skipping one or two at a time. He needed
to beat the deliveryman to the floor so he could scope it out and
see how viable his plan really was. It only took him two glances at
the signage to see that it would work.

Cal crouched in the doorway, two rooms down from Hernandez's room, awaiting the arrival of the room service meal.

One minute later, the young man Cal had paid off knocked on Hernandez's door.

"Room service," he announced.

"I didn't order anything," came the response from inside the room.

"Well, I've got a cheeseburger and fries with a drink for Room 552 on my ticket here."

No response. Then a few seconds later, the door unlocked and opened about a foot. Hernandez was standing on the other side, peering into the hallway. He took the meal inside and closed the door behind him.

Cal waited all of ten seconds, which seemed more like ten minutes. Hernandez opened the door and headed down the hallway in the opposite direction carrying the ice bucket. Cal pressed himself so hard against the doorway to hide himself he thought for sure he would leave an impression. He glanced down the hallway and Hernandez seemed unsuspecting of anyone out to get him. Cal had instructed the wait staff to serve a room temperature drink. It was Cal's long shot bet to get into the room and gain the upper hand.

When Hernandez rounded the corner, Cal dashed across the hall and jammed the key card he borrowed from the room service attendant into the slot above the door handle. The light turned green and Cal heard a click. He pushed down on the lever and rushed into the room.

Squirming in the corner was a boy, gagged and tied. Maybe he was 12 or 13 years old. He looked like he was from Latin America somewhere. Cal couldn't think fast enough to narrow it down to which country, nor could he have known for sure if he had a week to mull it over. All he had time to do was untie the boy and escape with their lives.

"It's OK. I'm gonna get you out of here," Cal said.

The boy grimaced and attempted to say something, though Cal

couldn't make it out. Cal decided the gag wasn't a priority at this point. He fumbled with the ropes, ripping the knot loose as fast as he could. Letting his instincts take over, Cal started at the boy's feet and moved to his hands. *Feet first because maybe he could run if necessary.* Cal then began working on the right hand then the left. He had just finished untying the boy when the door clicked. Cal froze.

Cal looked up to see Hernandez walk through the door carrying a bucket of ice. Hernandez immediately dropped the ice and went for his handgun tucked in the back of his pants. But Cal didn't give Hernandez time to pull it out. Instead, he rushed Hernandez. Hernandez, still fumbling for his gun, never had a chance to point in Cal's general direction. Cal sent Hernandez flying backward, slamming Hernandez's head into the room door. Hernandez dropped the gun as he slumped to the floor, attempting to fend off Cal. Cal slid the gun across the room with his foot as a fistfight commenced.

Cal moved closer to Hernandez, brooding over the man who still appeared stunned from what just happened. Cal balled up his fist and began pounding Hernandez's face. A left and then a right, followed by another right. It felt rhythmic to Cal—and therapeutic. Hernandez squirmed in an attempt to get free, but Cal was having none of it. Straddling the older man, Cal struck Hernandez over and over, each punch delivered with vengeful rage. Cal thought about scared little Jake each time—and now the latest victim Hernandez had terrorized in an effort to make money. Over and over again Cal punched until blood began to trickle out of Hernandez's mouth. Cal and his adrenaline wanted to keep going, but he couldn't. There was a line he wouldn't cross. Let the feds sort it out. Don't take a man's life, however pathetic it might have been. He wasn't a killer.

Cal stopped and looked at his tormentor, this tough powerful cartel leader who had been promptly neutered by a less-than imposing reporter. Hernandez looked beaten. He looked nearly immobile due to the punishment he had just received from Cal. He sat propped up against the wall, barely able to open his eyes.

Cal eased up and turned around toward the boy, who was now holding the gun. His hands trembled as he pointed it downward.

"We don't need that any more," Cal said, gesturing to the gun. It's going to be OK."

Instead, the boy raised the gun and pointed it in Cal's direction.

Bewildered, Cal held his hands up in surrendered. "It's OK. I'm here to help you. There's no need to shoot anybody."

But Cal never heard Hernandez getting up behind him. Hernandez pulled a knife out of his pocket and lunged toward Cal.

That's when the boy fired the gun.

Bam!

Just once was all it took. The boy fell back into his chair and dropped the gun. Cal spun to see Hernandez slump to the ground, blood oozing everywhere. The boy had shot Hernandez in the chest.

Cal gasped at the sight of Hernandez, writhing on the floor. He looked at the boy but didn't know what to say. Stepping on Hernandez's wrist, Cal slid the knife out of his hand with his other foot. Hernandez coughed up blood and looked helplessly up at Cal.

Cal got up and looked at the boy, who was still half enraged and half shocked at what had just happened.

"Are you OK?" Cal asked.

The boy nodded.

"What's your name?"

"Gio Gomez," he answered.

"Is your dad Brandon?"

The boy nodded again.

Then it all made sense to Cal. Brandon Gomez was the Seahawks' place kicker. As the team's quarterback, Noah Larson would have the biggest impact on the outcome of the game. But if the game was close, controlling the kicker was a best second option. Gomez had been perfect during the regular season on extra points, yet he missed one early in the Super Bowl. Cal now knew this was intentional. If the Seahawks trailed late in the game, all they would need would be a field goal to take the lead and win it. They wouldn't gamble, not with the Super Bowl on the line. Let Gomez boot them to victory.

Cal called his FBI contact and reported the news as he turned on the television.

"We've got Hernandez, but send an ambulance. He's barely alive," Cal said. "And we've got to get a message to Brandon Gomez that his son is safe."

As the picture on the television materialized, Cal realized Hernandez just might ruin the Super Bowl after all: The Seahawks trailed 21-20 with less than a minute to go and appeared to be content to set up a game winning field goal.

Hernandez slowly opened his eyes and glanced at the screen. Cal didn't really want to give Hernandez the pleasure of watching his plan come to fruition right before he died. He had to do something. With one eye on Hernandez, Cal didn't give up on getting word to Gomez that his son was safe. He wanted that call to be the last thing Hernandez heard.

The seconds ticked away on the clock. Cal called Josh. Surely he would pick up if he saw him calling and could get a message to someone. The phone rang and rang. No answer.

The Seahawks are just going to put this ball in the middle of the field and rely on the leg of Brandon Gomez to win Seattle's first Super Bowl title.

Cal looked at Gio.

"Can I call your mom? Do you think she can get a message to your dad?"

Gio shrugged. He was still visibly distraught.

"What's her number?"

Cal began dialing the numbers Gio relayed to him. But the phone just rang and rang. It went to voicemail. Cal told her that her son was safe and out of harm's way.

Then the FBI swat team arrived, storming into the room. They shoved their way past Cal and secured the room. Two paramedics began working on Hernandez while an FBI agent watched Hernandez intently. Cal acknowledged their presence but remained deep in thought as to how he could get the message to Gomez.

He began calling everyone he knew. AP sports writer Damon James would answer Cal's call. But nothing. Every reporter Cal knew was on deadline, predictably pounding out two different lead paragraphs for their story—one with Gomez making the kick and one with him missing it. All Gomez had to do was take the kick to fill in the blanks.

Seattle called timeout.

Cal continued wracking his brain for a solution. He called someone he knew from the NFL office. No answer. He called his editor. No answer. He called the phone in the press box. No answer. In desperation, he even tried Kelly. She didn't pick up either.

Well, this is it, folks. Once this timeout is over, Brandon Gomez has a chance to be the toast of Seattle. A 25-yard field goal and he will become as famous in Seattle as the Space Needle.

* * *

DURING THE TIMEOUT, Noah paced along on the sideline. He had done what was required of him—almost. In the playoff game the week before, the holder for Gomez had torn a hamstring in a freak mishap during practice, leaving Noah—the team's backup holder—as the second most important man on the field for the kick. All he had to do was get the ball down, tilt it back, laces out. He had done it a hundred times. He could do it blindfolded in his sleep. And if he could do it right one more time, he could put the week's terrible circumstances behind him and ride off into retirement as a Super Bowl champion. Maybe he'd go to Disney World. But there was no maybe about him retiring. He'd given his word to Ellen. This was it—win or lose.

If only it were that easy.

Noah looked at Gomez, who looked pale. Sweat was gushing down Gomez's face. But this was Texas in February—it wasn't hot. Noah had seen Gomez nervous before, but never like this. It seemed so uncharacteristic of Gomez that Noah wondered if he should mention something to his coach.

Throughout the course of the Seahawks' timeout, Noah's confidence in Gomez to make the easy kick went from a hundred percent to twenty-five percent. He almost thought about it being zero percent, but given a hundred kicks from this distance, even a nervous Gomez would stand to make a few.

The head official blew his whistle, urging the players to return to the field. Noah trotted to the huddle, one that was generally useless in most cases, but he used it as a way to instill confidence in everyone that Gomez could make this kick.

Noah gave a reassuring nod to Gomez as they broke the huddle.

CHAPTER 47

CAL NEVER STOPPED TRYING to reach someone. He punched in every number he could think of and dialed it just as fast. The Seahawks' media relations director. The cute sports reporter from Q13. The ESPN sports columnist he knew. Nobody answered.

Paramedics continued to work on Hernandez as the other FBI agents tried to piece together the recent events that led to their prime suspect with a serious bullet wound and bruises consistent with a fistfight. They asked Cal a few questions, but his answers were short and unhelpful. He knew that the Seahawks' kicker was walking onto the field with the ability to win the game—the Super Bowl!—but wouldn't because he thought his son would die if he made the kick. The drama unfolding in front of the world wasn't nearly as interesting to Cal. To him, it was like watching a bad ending to a movie for the second time.

Cal finally realized all he had was hope. He tossed his phone onto the bed and stared at the television screen. Ultimately, it didn't matter. None of it did. The only thing that was important was that two Seahawks' players wouldn't lose their sons over the terrible misfortune of making it to the Super Bowl. They would go on with their lives as families who avoided the worst of a nightmare no parent would wish on another. Cal did something good by stopping something bad. He stared down at Hernandez's body, which was still barely hanging on for life. Cal couldn't help but think in some way the villain still won, stealing something from every diehard Seahawks fan. Hernandez didn't see a single penny for his troubles, but the Seahawks were going to lose the Super Bowl on purpose.

The Seahawks line up for the kick, hoping to win the city of Seattle its first Super Bowl. Quarterback Noah Larson will be the holder and Brandon Gomez will take the kick. Here we go.

Cal couldn't look. He felt sick.

* * *

THIS WAS IT—Noah's personal raindrop moment. Random droplets colliding with one another, the outcome still in doubt. They splattered everywhere, nothing to control them. No one to control them. But Noah didn't want that. He didn't want to leave his fate to chance. Not today. Not when he could still do something about it.

When the center snapped the ball to Noah, he still wasn't sure if he had the nerve to do it. He just might be the biggest fool in the history of the Super Bowl. But he knew he couldn't let it end this way. Not with Gomez looking like he might vomit in the huddle. Not with all the people who depended upon him for leadership—and a victory. A shaken kicker with the yips? The city's shot at a title—and his own legacy—couldn't be determined by that. He didn't want to end his career as a loser. This was his moment and he was going to seize it.

Instead of putting the ball down, laces out, Noah scooped the ball up and took off running. He headed straight toward the near sideline and caught the entire Dolphins team off guard. It was a 25-yard field goal. Nobody ever suspected a fake, not even his own team.

The short run to the corner of the end zone felt like five minutes to Noah. The Dolphins' players realized what was happening, but only before it was too late. There were vain dives in Noah's direction. No one would catch him. No one would even touch him.

Noah couldn't believe the brilliance in his secret plan. No coach would ever have the nerve to make that call—and his didn't either. Who wouldn't put the odds on their kicker making one of the highest-percentage kicks in football? But Noah sensed the odds weren't good. So he did it. He took his raindrop and put it in a one place nobody could touch it.

He glanced at the referee straddling the goal line as he crossed it. His hands hoisted in the air, his mouth ready to blow the final whistle. *Touchdown!*

* * *

OH, MY! I don't believe it. The Seahawks are world champions with a touchdown off a 25-yard fake field goal! This might be the biggest surprise attack in American history since Washington crossed the Delaware! Seattle, it's time to celebrate!

Cal looked up and stared at the television in disbelief. *What? A fake field goal? Are you kidding me?*

Gomez's son started pumping his fist and shouting.

"Yes! Yes!" the boy shouted.

Cal saw the first flicker of life in the boy's eyes since they met all of twenty minutes ago. It was nice to see Gio be a kid after such a horrific experience.

Then Cal looked at Hernandez.

"You lost, Hernandez," Cal said. "Your little scheme got you nothing in the end."

Hernandez didn't respond to Cal. He closed his eyes and his body went limp. The paramedics began scrambling but there was nothing he could do. Hernandez was dead.

For about a minute, Cal stared at the now lifeless body of a man who was intent on ruining a family just so he could make some quick money. It was disgusting, evil really. But at least he hadn't

won today. And he'd never play this treacherous game with anyone else.

Cal turned his attention back toward the television and watched
the confetti cannons unleash their fury on Reliant Stadium, flut-
tering down upon the exuberant Seahawks team and the devas-
tated Dolphins. He knew it would be all but gone once he arrived
at the stadium, but he had to go there tonight. Now.

"Let's get you home, kid," Cal said.

Gomez's son nodded and smiled.

"Is it OK if I take him back to his parents?" Cal asked one of
the FBI agents.

"Sure, Cal. We'll send an agent with you and get statements
from both of you later."

That was all Cal needed to hear. The happy pair maneuvered
around the busy hive of agents cataloging the scene. Nobody really cared how or why Hernandez died, just that he was dead. And
Cal wasn't interested in sticking around for more bureaucratic paperwork and questioning. He had experienced plenty of that in
the past few days. It was time to reunite a son with his father—
and celebrate a Super Bowl victory.

As they were walking out the door, Cal heard a cell phone ring.
Just background noise. He ignored it. Until he heard something
one of the agents said: "The dead man's phone is ringing."

Cal wanted to stop and find out who it was, but one of the
agents looked up at Cal and said, "We'll handle it, Mr. Murphy.
You've got more important things to do."

Cal froze. *Hernandez wasn't calling the shots!*

CHAPTER 48

LONGSHORE AND THE OTHER security agents watched their mystery man as the game came to its dramatic conclusion. He seemed agitated at first and then became enraged. He dialed a number on his cell phone but no one answered. He held a cane, but he walked as if it didn't need it. The man paced throughout the sports book before storming toward the black jack tables. Then chaos.

He took his cane and slamming it on black jack and poker tables, raked all the players' cards onto the floor. Chips were strewn everywhere.

"Get him now!" Longshore yelled as security personnel scrambled across the floor toward the epicenter of the man's tirade.

Then he moved to another table and then another. Women screamed and fled their tables. A couple of men tried to subdue him, but the man promptly whacked them and marched to his next target.

It took three security guards to tackle and pin the man down. But not before he had wreaked more havoc than Longshore had ever seen while working at the Oasis. Security guards zip tied the man and escorted him off the floor.

Once off the main floor, Longshore stopped the guards.

Longshore spoke first. "Well, Mr. Nixon. You made quite a

scene tonight. Needless to say, you'll never darken the door of this casino ever again. You understand?"

The man kept his head down, unwilling to look at Longshore.

"But before you leave, let's find out who you really are."

Longshore walked behind the man and fished out his wallet. He walked back in front of the man and tried to compare his face with the one depicted on his driver's license. The man looked up for a brief moment and put his head back down.

"Yep, that's you all right. The media is going to love this story."

Longshore shoved the man's wallet into his chest and continued.

"You ought to be ashamed of what you did," Longshore said. "And I'm not talking about what went on here tonight."

Finally the man broke his silence. "I don't know what you're talking about."

"Oh, I think you do. And I think that I'm wasting my breath telling you not to come back here. You'll be lucky if you get to see the light of day again, much less a casino in Vegas. And trust me when I say this: This isn't staying in Vegas."

Longshore stared in disgust at the man. "Get him outta here!"

He turned and watched the security guards march the man away. Longshore knew he'd be seeing the man's face on television every day for the next three months, if not more.

* * *

CAL LEFT THE SCENE with Gio and another FBI agent, questions swirling in his mind. *If Hernandez wasn't behind this scheme, then who was? Who would go to those lengths to hire him? Who needed money that bad? Or worse, who hated Noah Larson and Brandon Gomez?* Those questions would have to wait.

Cal mulled over the facts as they headed downstairs. In the lobby, the bar patrons buzzed over the game's ending. It was an unlikely one for sure, and it irked Cal that he wasn't writing about it. A few rowdy Seahawks fans enjoyed taunting the miserable

Miami fans. To be so close yet to lose? It was the worst agony any fan could know. But Cal knew nothing of it tonight, for this was his chance to celebrate, to put aside his objectivity for a moment and soak in the exhilarating feeling of having his favorite NFL team take the world title.

The agent driving zoomed Cal and Gio toward the stadium. A flashing light in the windshield parted a sea of cars at every congested area.

Cal looked at Gio and stopped thinking about football for a moment. Instead, he thought about how scared the kid next to him must have been—so scared that he shot his kidnapper. Cal wanted to forget what had just happened. He wanted to wish it away, cover it up with a mental white sheet and never show it the light of day. But no matter how traumatic his past few days had been, it surely didn't compare to Jake's or Gio's experience. Nabbed by a filthy stranger. Threatened at gunpoint. Separated from your family. No one deserved this, especially not a kid. Not Jake. Not Gio. Not anyone.

"You want to talk about what happened?" Cal asked.

Gio gazed out the window.

"I understand if you don't. I just thought you might want to."

Finally, Gio said something, his voice quivering. "What do you want to know?"

Cal paused. "What did they do to you? Did they hurt you?"

"No."

"Did they try to scare you?"

"Yeah."

"Did you think they were going to kill you?"

Gio nodded.

"How old are you? Twelve?"

"Thirteen."

"No thirteen-year-old boy should have to go through what you just went through."

Then Gio began sobbing, heaving as he let loose his suppressed emotions.

"It's OK, Gio. You're OK now."

Gio continued crying for another minute before he regained his composure.

"I think what you did today was very brave. Who knows what might have happened had that man stabbed me with a knife."

Gio nodded.

"Where did you learn to shoot like that?"

"I visit my cousins every summer in Colombia—and you need to know how to defend yourself there. My dad taught me how to shoot a gun. I never thought I would have to shoot another person."

Gio then buried his head in his hands. Occasional sniffles broke the otherwise thick silence in the car.

Cal took a deep breath and ran his hands through his hair. He didn't like the idea of being a vigilante and getting his own justice, but in a way he was relieved. He knew Hernandez would've likely hunted him his whole life. But not now. Almost the entire cartel had been wiped out earlier in the day, but it was a 13-year-old kid who unwittingly cut the head off the snake.

As he stared at the fragile boy sharing the backseat with him, Cal wondered what effect this experience would have on Gio. Would it harden him? Send him into a depression? Hopefully, he would recover from this event in his life and be a better person for it. Cal could only hope for the best.

In the distance, Cal saw the lights glowing from the stadium. It seemed like he was re-entering some alternate reality after being entrenched in the real world—a hard world—for the past few days.

Cal's team had escaped with a Super Bowl victory, but Cal had escaped with something much more important. He had escaped with his life, a fact that helped him put everything back into perspective.

The car came to a stop and the agent opened the door for the boy. Cal got out and joined them as they all rushed through security and a sea of jubilant Seahawks fans and depressed Dolphin fans exiting the stadium en masse.

A few pieces of confetti trickled from the upper reaches of the stadium toward the field as Cal walked through the tunnel with Gio. Apparently, no one had notified Gomez of the events over the past hour. Several Seattle players had yet to walk off the field, hoping to hold onto the moment just a little bit longer. But not Gomez. He sat on the end of a bench with his heads buried in his hands. His helmet rested between his feet on the ground as he shook and sobbed. Almost anyone else taking in this scene would have assumed they were tears of joy.

When Gio realized his father was crying, his brisk walking pace turned into a full sprint.

"Daaaad!" he yelled.

Gomez looked up, mouth agape. A grin then spread across his face as he ran toward Gio before embracing him. More tears from Gomez. Then Gio broke too. Their hug seemed to last for over a minute, their voices breaking as they shared their joy.

Cal took it all in from 30 yards away, folding his arms and watching with satisfaction. *This beats the winning moment of the Super Bowl.* And not a soul was watching them but Cal. He knew he would never what the Gomez family had been through, but Cal did know what it was like to almost lose someone you care about.

* * *

IN THE TUNNEL beneath the stadium, reporters crowded around the 30-plus podiums set up for the players to answer questions. A few of the podiums were larger than others with more space for journalists to gather. Noah Larson stood behind one of those podiums.

"How does it feel to finally get the stigma off your back of being one of the league's best quarterbacks without a Super Bowl title?" asked one of the reporters.

"Well, I know you guys all talk about that stuff, but even if we had lost tonight, it wouldn't have changed how I felt about my career. I've worked hard and did my best every time I stepped on the field. And that's not always good enough. There are plenty of guys in this league who work hard but never win a Super Bowl. That shouldn't change how they are viewed. It's hard to get here once, let alone twice."

"Was that fake field goal called by the coaches?" another reporter asked.

"Absolutely not." Noah laughed. So did the reporters. But Noah knew it wouldn't have been a laughing matter if he didn't score on the play.

"So, what possessed you to take off with the ball like that?" another reporter asked.

"To be honest, I love Gomez. He's done a great job all year long for us and if it wasn't for him, we wouldn't have won a few close games. But I just had a feeling and I went with it. It's a play we practice, but one that was never called. Fortunately it worked out for us tonight."

"Did any of the coaches say anything to you after that?"

"Yeah, something like, 'We're Super Bowl champions!'"

More laughs erupted from the reporters.

"Earlier you said if you lost it wouldn't have changed how you felt about your career, speaking in the past tense. Are you considering retirement?" one of the reporters questioned.

"Well, I didn't want to steal any thunder from our team tonight by announcing this, but yes. That was my last game. I promised my wife before the game, so that was it either way."

Noah stared into the blinding camera lights. Photographers' cameras began flashing. He could feel the pool of reporters swelling as a buzz hummed around the open area near his podium. Noah sipped his bottled water and waited in silence for the next question.

"Why now?" one of the reporters asked. "You just had one of the best seasons of your career and you just won the Super Bowl. Don't you feel like you could keep doing this for a few more years?"

"Sure, I could. But it's a few more years I would miss out on getting to be there for my family. Look, I've had to work hard to get where I am, and it's only going to require a greater commitment as I get older. But I love my family more than anything in the world, including football. And quite frankly, I'd rather spend my time with them moving forward than studying film."

Noah looked off to the side of the podium and saw Jake with Ellen. He motioned for Jake to join him. Without hesitating, Jake scampered over to his dad and plopped into his lap. Suddenly, a new flurry of flashes exploded in the room.

"You don't think you'll reconsider retirement?" one reporter asked.

"Absolutely not. I gave my wife my word—and you don't know my wife." Noah's remark drew some chuckles. Then he continued. "I love Seattle and the fans here have been great. And tonight was what the past ten years have been about, getting to this point. But this franchise has some great young talent and it's time for me to get out of the way and let somebody else have the spotlight."

An NFL media relations personnel announced that there would be no more questions for Noah. He walked toward Ellen and gave her a big hug.

"Convinced this is it?" he asked.

"Well, you've convinced me," she said, smiling. "Do you think you even have a chance of backing out now?"

"I wouldn't think about it—besides, I meant every word I said up there."

Ellen hugged him again.

An NFL employee then tapped Noah on the shoulder. "Mr. Larson, a Cal Murphy said he needed to speak with you. Is it OK if you speak with him?"

"Sure," Noah said, spinning around and seeing Cal.

Cal approached the Larsons.

"Cal, how can I ever thank you enough for what you did?" Noah asked.

"Well, an exclusive would be nice," Cal said, smiling.

"Anything you want."

"Seriously, I'm glad I could help. I would hope someone else would do that for me one day if necessary." Cal looked down and rubbed Jake on the head.

"I just can't thank you enough."

"Well, I'll call you tomorrow and get your side of the story for this article. But before I go and let you get back with your family here, I need to tell you that Hernandez wasn't really behind all this."

"No? Who was?"

"I'm not sure yet, but I know there was someone else."

"Well, are we safe? I don't know. You'll have to talk to somebody with the FBI about that. But be careful, OK?"

Noah nodded. He shook Cal's hand and turned toward Ellen and Jake, pulling them in tightly.

CHAPTER 49

CAL WALKED BACK TOWARD THE MEDIA TENT and called Kelly.

"Are you still here?" Cal asked as she answered.

"You made it?"

"Not until it was over, but I'm here now."

"Wasn't that amazing?! I still can't believe it!"

"I know. Absolutely incredible. I'll have to tell you the rest of the story some time."

"OK. It'll have to be tomorrow. I'm sure you have work to do and I've got a party to go to."

Cal was silent.

"Cal, are you OK? You're acting a little funny."

"Well, it's just that I miss you. I can't thank you enough for what you did in Mexico. I think I'd be dead. And you? You saved a little boy's life."

"I'm no hero, Cal. I just did what needed to be done."

"I know, but I couldn't help but think how things could have gone differently—and gone really wrong."

"Yeah, let's not talk about that, OK? They didn't, so we're good. All right?"

"It's just that I wouldn't ever want anything to happen to you, Kelly."

"Are you getting all soft on me, Cal Murphy?"

Cal took a deep breath. "I just really care about you."

"I know you do. I care about you, too. I'm glad you're safe."

"Me too."

"When are you leaving?"

"Tuesday at noon. It was the earliest flight out of here I could get."

"Same here."

"Want to meet me for breakfast on Tuesday?"

"Sure. I'll call you and we can make plans."

"Sounds great. Take care."

Cal hung up. He immediately began to regret his failing courage. He wanted to tell Kelly how he really felt, that he saw their relationship as more than just friends. But he couldn't. And he couldn't figure out why either.

* * *

CAL ARRIVED AT THE MEDIA TENT and scanned the area for Josh. He spotted him in the far corner, pecking away on his keyboard. He walked up to Josh, out of his line of sight.

"What are you writing about, rookie?" Cal asked close to Josh's ear.

Josh turned around, startled.

"I'm writing a sidebar on the fake field goal. How are you? I see you made it back in one piece. What'd the other guy look like?"

Cal just now realized that his appearance was disheveled, not to mention his face held several visible cuts and bruises. "You don't want to know. But I'm here and all accounted for."

"That's good. How did your little assignment with the FBI go? I'm assuming that's where you got your little scratches from."

Cal smiled. "It ended well."

"That's good." Josh pounded away on his laptop for a few more seconds before speaking again. "By the way, were you trying to reach me near the end of the game? What was so important that you couldn't wait?"

"Why didn't you pick up?"

"I was down on the field and had my phone in my pocket. It was deafening down there. I guess I didn't hear it ring. What did you want?"

"Oh, nothing now. It's fine."

"Good. Well, let's talk later after I'm off of deadline, OK?"

"Sounds good."

Just then Cal's phone rang.

It was Agent Anderson.

CHAPTER 50

"JARRETT! HOW ARE YOU?" Cal asked as he answered his phone.

"Fine. And you?"

"Wonderful. I'm alive."

"That's good news. Well, since you helped us out, you get some privileged information first. We found out there was someone else behind everything."

"No kidding?"

Cal was half joking, half playing coy. He wanted Anderson to feel like he was giving him some information that nobody knew but him. A person feels more comfortable about sharing juicy details if he thinks he's the only one who knows them. It was a little interviewing trick he learned that always helped him get those extra details that nobody else could get.

"Nope. And I wish I was, too. This is pretty unbelievable."

"Oh? Who was it? Would I know the person?"

"Probably not, but you'd know his son. A guy by the name of Trent Newton. His son Hunter plays quarterback for the Dolphins. Ever heard of him?"

"Hunter Newton's dad? No way! You've got to be kidding me! How did you discover this?"

"Well, it's crazy, but one of the casino's security detail had been watching this guy for the past few days. He plunked down 100Gs on the Dolphins to win. Nobody knew who he was at first because he checked in under an alias and was wearing a disguise."

"Seriously?"

"Yeah, one of the security guys eventually recognized him but they didn't say anything to him. Then when Seattle scored at the end, he went crazy. He started destroying some of the Oasis' black jack tables with a cane. It was crazy."

"So, then what happened?"

"Well, after their security team apprehended him and ushered him off the floor, we entered the scene and are dealing with him now."

"Did he happen to make any calls after the game?"

"As a matter of fact, he did. According to the phone records stored on his phone, it didn't look like anybody answered—and supposedly that's when he went crazy."

"OK, thanks so much. Can I print this?"

"Sure, just call me tomorrow to confirm and make sure that everything I said is able to be released to the public."

"You got it."

* * *

CAL HAILED A CAB and headed back to his hotel. He had a story to write, one that made the articles being pounded out on deadline by a tent full of serious reporters seem like the Sunday comics in comparison. They wrote about a game; he was going to write about the biggest scandal in sports history since Shoeless Joe and the White Sox threw the 1919 World Series.

He texted Solterbeck.

Have you talked to the office in Vegas? Check Hernandez's phone for the last call. See if it was from Trent Newton. Talk in the morning?

Cal waited a few seconds for Solterbeck's reply.

Thanks for the tip. Will look into it. I'll call you at 10 am.

Cal clicked his phone off and slumped into the back seat of the cab. He needed some rest.

CHAPTER 51

CAL WANTED TO GO TO SLEEP. It was nearly midnight by the time he reached his room and the morning would come early. But he couldn't go to sleep. Not with all the plotlines for the story he would write pinging around in his mind.

One father was willing to give up his dream—his legacy—for his son's life. Another father was intent on kidnapping an innocent child to ensure his son would be hailed as a hero. Cal knew this Super Bowl would forever be remembered by what he would write the next morning, not for the dramatic ending.

But this was the ending Cal wanted to write about, the one where good overcame evil. It was the one where the reckless actions of many were negated by the good actions of a few.

When Cal pondered all the facts of the story—especially the latest one, that Newton's dad directed the Mexican cartel to ensure his son would win the Super Bowl by means of kidnapping family members of the opposing teams' key players—the words of the Juarez priest stuck with him:

We, who question, have no way of knowing the full story.

Cal knew the full story wasn't written. Who knew how this horrific event might change the course of these families' lives? Maybe it would even be for the best. Maybe not. But this chapter was written. Done. Finished. And evil didn't win. Justice did. Two kids slept at home with their dads tonight, right where they should be. Cal didn't know the full story. Nobody did. But this piece of it was a satisfying one. It was a good thought to drift asleep to.

CHAPTER 52

THE NEXT MORNING, Cal awoke an hour before Solterbeck was scheduled to call him. He showered and shaved before going downstairs to eat breakfast. Over a plate of scrambled eggs and toast, Cal read the *Houston Chronicle's* rendition of the fantastic finish to the Super Bowl. The paper's columnist hailed the play as one of the greatest in Super Bowl history and called Noah Larson the gutsiest quarterback in the NFL. Cal smiled as he read the praise heaped upon Seattle's quarterback. The man deserved every word of it.

He returned upstairs to get his computer ready for his interview with Solterbeck.

At 10 a.m. sharp, Solterbeck called Cal.

"You doing all right?" Solterbeck asked.

"All things considered, I guess I am."

"Good. Thanks for your tip last night. You were right. Trent Newton called Hernandez right after the game. That was all we needed to make the link. He'll be going away for a long time. We've charged him with extortion, kidnapping, and accessory to murder."

"Wow. I can't believe this."

"Yeah, it's quite shocking."

"What other questions do you have for me?"

Cal knew every detail of the case, but he needed to get Solterbeck to say it on record so he could write it. It felt strange to Cal, but it needed to be done so his editors wouldn't nix anything about this story. He knew it intimately but needed to do his due diligence as a journalist, a lost art among the majority of his peers.

After the interview, Cal didn't leave his room. He called Noah and got a few comments from him and his perspective on the story. He gathered a handful of other sources and commenced writing the piece.

In the past, Cal wrote a few articles that earned him national writing awards. There was no doubt this one would land him in the public spotlight for breaking the biggest sports story of the past century. But none of the accolades would compare to the moment he reunited Gio with his father or saw Noah with Jake for the first time after the kidnapping.

* * *

EARLY THAT AFTERNOON, Cal finished writing his story and emailed it to his editors. What he uncovered in further research and talking with sources was an unlikely and convoluted plot that nearly cost two kids their lives. One of the biggest questions Cal wanted to know was how in the world did Trent Newton meet up with a drug cartel lord? Newton had no record to speak of, according to FBI sources. It wasn't like he could've just looked him up in the phone book under "Extortionist for Hire." Then Cal discovered that Newton ran a food distribution business, one that had a contract to provide various restaurants and grocery store chains with *Buenisimo!* coffee. With that piece of information, Cal connected all the dots and wrote another award-winning investigative piece. It was a story that people would talk about for years to come.

It didn't take long for Fink to write him back.

Wow! This is incredible reporting!

Cal smiled. He would have preferred to simply write about an unlikely fake that won the Seahawks the Super Bowl. But he'd settle for a compliment like that from Fink, something that was tougher to get than a Pulitzer Prize.

* * *

THE NEXT MORNING, Cal went downstairs early to the lobby for breakfast with Kelly. He arrived well before she did so he could watch television. He mostly wanted to hear if his name was being tossed around on SportsCenter like it was familiar to everyone.

"The Seattle Times' Cal Murphy broke one of the biggest stories in the last century today when he revealed the details behind a plot to have the outcome of the Super Bowl manipulated by kidnapping two players' sons. In his piece published today, Murphy revealed that the players who were involved were indeed Seattle quarterback Noah Larson and kicker Brandon Gomez. However, both players' sons were rescued by FBI initiatives before the game was over, ensuring that the integrity of the outcome remained intact.

Cal chuckled. He knew that last bit was only technically true. Regardless of the way others in the media were relating his story, it was still fun to hear him talked about on his favorite ESPN show.

"What are you laughing at, Mr. Famous Sportswriter?" Kelly asked as she slid out her chair and joined Cal.

"Oh, just how people like to misconstrue facts to make a better story."

"Really? People do that?"

Cal sensed Kelly's sarcastic wit right away.

He played along. "Yeah. Can you believe it?"

"Well, congratulations, Cal. You deserve every award you get for this story."

"Too bad you can't get one too."

"True. But I think we both know that stuff isn't really important, is it?"

Cal paused. He took a deep breath. If Noah Larson could fake a field goal to win a Super Bowl surely he could grit his teeth and say what needed to be said.

"About that, Kelly. I think you're right and this whole ordeal really got me thinking about what is most important to me."

Cal's words hung in the air as Kelly patiently waited for more.

"And when I thought about what is most important to me, my mind kept coming back to you. If anything would've happened to you down there in Mexico, I don't know what I would've done. The truth is I feel more courageous when I'm with you, like I can do anything no matter what the circumstances."

He paused, hoping Kelly would say something—anything—to help him ease his discomfort at the moment. But she said nothing, so he continued.

"I know I've told you before that I really care about you. And I really do. I really really care about you. More so than just being adventure buddies, if you know what I mean?"

Kelly finally spoke. "What do you mean, Cal?"

"What I mean is that I think we ought to give this thing a chance, you know—us."

Kelly reached across the table and grabbed one of Cal's trembling hands.

"Cal, I felt the same way when you didn't make it out with me and Jake. All I could think about was how horrible it would be if I never saw you again."

Cal smiled and sighed. He could relax. The chance of rejection had vanished.

"Well, maybe we'll have to find jobs in the same city this time and figure this thing out. What do you say?"

"I did just get an offer to move to San Francisco to be the bureau's assistant photo editor."

"San Francisco, huh?"

"Yeah, San Francisco. I bet they might have room on staff for an award-winning sports writer there."

Cal turned red. He didn't mind compliments from most people, but for some reason, Kelly heaping praise on him always felt a little awkward.

"I'll have to look into that," he said.

They finished their breakfast as news of the story Cal broke served as the looping background noise on every cable news and sports television station. Cal helped save Seattle's Super Bowl, but he was confident now that he wouldn't be there for much longer.

CHAPTER 53

NOAH SQUINTED AS HE looked up at the sky. Confetti mixed with rain pelted him as the Seahawks' parade rolled through downtown Seattle on a nasty Wednesday morning. Fans cheered and chanted his name. It was as if the entire parade was for him. By now, they all knew the story. Not just that he had gambled the Super Bowl title on that one play, but that he spent an entire week worrying about his son.

Every media outlet already wanted the renegade quarterback on their shows that week—then Cal's story hit the newsstands and Internet two days after the Super Bowl. Noah preferred to stay at home with his family. But at their urging, he decided to appear on a few shows that wanted to fly him out with the stipulation that his whole family's flights must be covered as well. Those interviews were still a couple of days away.

But none of that fame mattered much to Noah. He hugged his son tightly and soaked in the final moment of adulation over his career. Noah didn't feel like he thought he would a week ago if Seattle achieved a victory. He felt sorry for breaking the city's budget because of the parade, though he knew no one would care. Noah didn't want this moment to be vindictive in any way. He wanted it to be cherished. So cherish it he did with Jake.

As the motorcade reached 12th Street, the Seahawks' 12th Man club chanted Noah's name. One member of the club took a microphone and recited a special poem he wrote to honor Noah and his short touchdown run. Noah smiled at the gesture and waved to the 12th Man club.

With the parade winding down, Jake looked up at Noah and asked, "Dad, do you think we can go to a few Sounders games this year now that you're retired?"

"I doubt it, Jake."

He paused and watched the grin vanish off Jake's face.

"I don't think we can go to a *few* Sounders game," Noah said. "I think we should go to *all* of their games."

Jake hugged Noah and started jumping up and down.

"You want to get season tickets?" Noah asked.

"Yes! Oh, daddy, I love you so much!"

Noah smiled. He would miss the touchdowns, the roar of the crowd, the camaraderie with his teammates. But none of that compared to the moment he just experienced—a great big hug from his son and realizing that he was his hero. Noah no longer felt the need to convert Jake into a football fan. Jake was his No. 1 fan and that's all that mattered.

* * *

BACK HOME IN SEATTLE, Cal watched the parade on the newsroom television. Someone else could write that sappy feel-good parade story.

"Good work, Cal," Fink said, joining Cal in watching a parade they both never thought they would see.

"Thanks."

"You did good. I know you saw some crazy stuff down there, but you're a bigger man than I am. And you won't be here long if other editors think you'll go to any extremes to get a good story."

Cal smiled. "Well, it wasn't supposed to be that extreme. I'll tell you that much. I would've never gone if I thought any of that stuff was going to happen."

"Yeah, you would've. Cal, you're a real newsman. Your nose for a story is something special."

Fink never praised his writers like this and Cal knew it. Another compliment from Fink? Now this one was almost as good as a five-figure Christmas bonus.

Fink patted Cal on the back and walked off without another word.

Cal turned his attention back to the television. He smiled as the camera zoomed in on Noah sharing a hug with his son. The past few days made him question his own judgment. Who thinks they can waltz into the home of one of the most dangerous cartel members in the world and it not be a big deal? Cal began to wonder if he was crazy. Had he lost his mind? Was his nose for news going to be the death of him? Life was about moments like the one he was witnessing on television—a father and a son connecting. It wasn't about some adrenaline rush that accompanied bringing down the bad guys.

Cal needed to be careful. He wanted some of those father-son moments in his future, the kind he hardly had a chance to have with his own dad. As a seven-year-old kid, Cal endured some of the worst pain in his life when his dad died. His mom remarried a few years later, but it wasn't the same. No stepdad could replace his dad. His dad had been a reporter too—and later Cal learned that his dad's editor suspected that his death had something to do with a story he had been working on. According to the editor, it wasn't a story Cal's dad had been assigned either.

Cal knew the same fate awaited him if he didn't change the reckless way he lived. So what if Fink just gave him the rarest of compliments. Cal had to stop charging to the rescue, even if it was to help somebody who needed his help. He had to realize he couldn't save everyone. And now there was Kelly to think about. She might be a bigger part of his future than he ever imagined. *Just stick to covering games and writing features on famous sports athletes and you can have a life like Noah's.* It was a nice thought.

The rain whipped against the newsroom office, a thousand raindrops fated to crash into an office window with no idea of what their future held.

THE END

ACKNOWLEDGEMENTS

We write in community and there have been plenty of people who have contributed to this project in one form or another.

Many thanks must first go to my dad, who taught me how to tell a good story, leaving me on the edge of my bed wanting the next snippet of his creative bedtime stories, and my mom, who instilled in me the importance of good grammar to accentuate good written stories.

I also want to thank Tim Booth, whose insights into Seattle sports scene helped craft the fine details in this manuscript.

I appreciate the editorial assistance of Jennifer Wolf and her keen eye in making this book better than it was.

And last but not least, I appreciate my wife for giving me the time to help make this book a reality.

ABOUT THE AUTHOR

JACK PATTERSON is an award-winning journalist living in southeastern Idaho with his wife and three children. He likes enjoying the great outdoors of the Northwest and following sports. He also loves connecting with readers and would love to hear from you. To stay updated about future projects, connect with him over Facebook at facebook.com/JackPattersonAuthor, on the Internet at www.IamJackPatterson.com or on Twitter at twitter.com/MrJackPatterson

Also by JACK PATTERSON ...

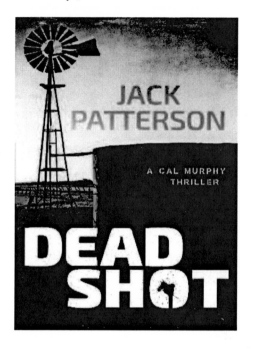

Working as a journalist at a small weekly paper in rural Idaho, Cal Murphy begins losing his big city dreams of writing for a metro paper before his passion is reignited after three high school star athletes are found dead in a 24-hour period.

As he and fellow photographer Kelly Mendoza attempt to make sense of bizarre circumstances that led to the teens' deaths, Cal makes a chilling discovery, uncovering a vast conspiracy that grows darker with every twist and turn.

With a mastermind determined to silence Cal and Kelly for good, the young reporters ultimately must decide if their lives are worth the risk to reveal the truth.

AVAILABLE at Amazon.com and other bookstores